TRUTH'S BLADE
THE RISING WAVE

MICHELLE DIENER

Cover design by: Creative Paramita

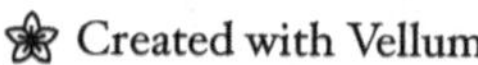 Created with Vellum

THE RISING WAVE SERIES

The Rising Wave (Prequel Novella)
The Turncoat King
The Threadbare Queen
Fate's Arrow
Truth's Blade

ABOUT TRUTH'S BLADE

A warrior enslaved . . .

Theo has been bested. On the hunt for missing children, he encounters a man who has more magical weapons than Theo could ever believe existed. And their confrontation may have ended with Theo managing to wound the abductor, but it leaves him spelled in the shape of a goat.

A woman trapped . . .

Melodie has been living a half-life in Illoa—exploited by her boss, restless at the thought of continuing on her current path, she stumbles into a situation she knows will change her life. When her ability to see spell work, which has led to a life in the shadows, allows her to see a man caged by magic, she has no hesitation in releasing him.

A partnership made in desperation . . .

When Theo asks her to help him find missing children, to go up against a spell worker who sounds like everything her deceased father tried to protect her from, Melodie accepts. She is tired of keeping herself safe at the expense of the truth, and Theo swears he will be the blade at her back.

But neither of them know the danger they will be facing, and how deep a bond they will have to forge with each other to fight an opponent with a heart this dark.

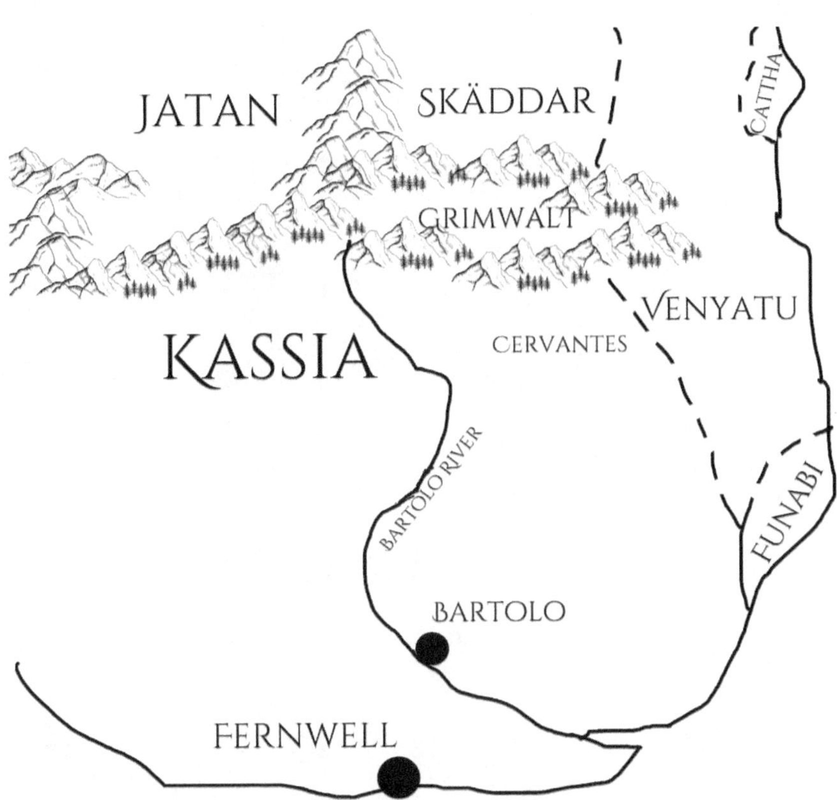

JATAN
SKÄDDAR
CATTHA
GRIMWALT
VENYATU
KASSIA
CERVANTES
BARTOLO RIVER
FUNABI
BARTOLO
FERNWELL

JATAN
SKÄDDAR
MIRROR MOUNTAINS
DALLIR RIVER
WALDRAND
TAUNEN
GRIMWALT
RIVER FEI
ILLOA
MALIN RIVER
VENYATU
KASSIA
N
W
E
S

CHAPTER 1

He had lost his charges.

Theo stared at the wreck that had been the novices' camp site. The only conclusion he could draw was that they had been taken, and violently.

He lifted two fingers to his lips and gave a high, loud whistle. The noise caused his horse to shake its head and he patted its neck in apology and dismounted, forcing himself to take in as much detail as he could as he worked out what had happened.

Here, Ricardo had stabbed his attacker. Theo studied the blood that stained the sharp end of one of the sticks Ric was always whittling by the fire.

Here, Genevieve had tried to use the leather sling she kept in her pocket at all times. The stone lay not far from the sling, so it had most likely been knocked out of her hand.

Theo bent and picked up both stone and sling and slid it into the bag he carried across his chest.

He turned at the sound of hooves, caught sight of his uncle, and went back to analyzing the scene.

Four children, out for a week on the plains, in what was to be their first taste of what it meant to be Cervantes, with him and his uncle camped nearby in case they needed help.

And they had been taken.

It was a nightmare that held the echoes of the past.

Of the days when young Cervantes—the younger the better—had been stolen by the Kassian queen and put into the diabolically named Chosen Camps.

Theo had been lucky to have never experienced that.

His uncle, who was dismounting behind him and cursing at the sight of the camp, knew about being taken all too well. He had been one of the Chosen. Had fought his way out of captivity by their leader's side, and had overcome their enemy.

Luc Franck, and his uncle Rafe, had managed to turn the tables on the Kassian army. They had fought back, and they had won.

"This is bad," Rafe said. He bent on one knee, thrusting his hand into the dead coals of the small camp fire. "There's a tiny bit of heat left in there," he said. "They've got five or six hours on us."

He stood suddenly, and for a moment, Theo thought he would have to catch his uncle before he fell.

"This can't be happening again." Rafe swayed, then snapped straight. "All of them are gone?"

"I'm about to check the perimeter. See if any of them managed to escape and hide." Theo realized he was speaking as if soothing a wild horse.

Rafe nodded, then blundered into the bush. Theo stared after him, at the sight of a man in panic. A man who'd never been anything but calm and thoughtful.

Theo took the opposite direction, hoping at least one of his students got away, but not expecting it.

They met back at the camp, and Theo studied Rafe before he swung back into the saddle. "I found tracks. They brought a cart to transport the children."

Rafe didn't answer. He stood, fists clenched and head bowed.

Theo needed to snap him out of this. Needed him to go for help while Theo chased after his charges.

"Question is, is this a repeat of the past, or is this an attack on the Commander and the queen?" he asked.

Rafe lifted his head. "No one knew Vivi would be here. No one."

Theo tilted his head. "That's not true."

"No stranger," Rafe amended. "No one who would wish the princess harm."

"I'd like to believe this is random chance, not a terrible replay of past wrongs, but we also need to consider whether it was a targeted attack on the crown, instead. Viviane *is* the princess. And she was taken." Theo's mount danced under him, feeling the tension. "I'm going after them. You need to get back to Ta-lin and raise the alarm."

His uncle started to shake his head, and Theo cut him off with a flick of his hand.

"There's no time to argue. I'm five hours behind as it is, and I'm faster than you are. Gather up their things and go for help." He didn't wait for a reply, he turned his horse and raced for the small gap in the greenery where he'd caught sight of deep cart wheel impressions.

At least they were alive when they left, Theo thought as he raced along the path the cart had carved into the plain. There was no sign of blood, other than on the end of Ricardo's stick.

He refused to consider there were ways of killing that didn't require the spilling of blood.

These were children. Cervantes children.

Just like the children who had been the focus of kidnap long ago.

Someone had foolishly decided to try it again.

All children were precious to the Cervantes. It wouldn't have mattered to the rescue mission whether the princess was one of their number or not. But she was.

And Theo looked forward to meeting up with their abductor.

Very much.

CHAPTER 2

THEO CREPT a little deeper under the bush, and at last he could see most of the camp.

He had followed the cart tracks to a road, and guessing the abductors wouldn't be headed south, deeper into Cervantes territory, where they would be surrounded by angry warriors, Theo had turned north, toward the Grimwalt border.

Hours later, long after dusk, the sight of a campfire glow off the road, and cart tracks digging into soft soil toward a small copse, had elated him.

He had left his horse near the road and ventured toward the camp on foot, finding a bush to take cover in while he sized up the situation.

The fire was dancing merrily, but the whole scene was eerily quiet. Bodies lay around the fire, and at first his heart jerked in his chest at their stillness, but after a moment he noticed the few who were facing his way were trussed up tight, with gags around their mouths. Some lay with their backs to him, but now his panic had cleared, he could see the bindings around their arms and hands, legs and feet.

All four were accounted for.

Ricardo, Jonquil, Genevieve, and Viviane.

He felt the first easing of the fear he'd been fighting since he'd come across their empty camp.

They were alive and he had eyes on them.

He could work with those circumstances.

He drew in a deep breath of relief.

Then he studied the camp layout.

The children were placed around the fire in a curiously equidistant manner, as if the person who had laid them down had measured the distance between each one to make sure it was exactly the same.

That worried Theo.

It smacked of spell work or a disturbed mind.

The cart that he'd been following was parked off to the side, the horse hobbled and left to graze.

There was no sign of the driver.

He had been operating under the assumption there was more than one person involved in the abduction, because while his students were only thirteen, they were Cervantes warriors in training, and no one would find them easy prey.

But the way they were laid out brought the possibility of spell work into things, and he conceded a powerful spell caster could have managed it alone.

He also sensed a trap. He could almost hear someone whispering, *'Here they are, come and get them.'*

He slowly backed out of the bush and rose to his feet, moving to the right, using the bushes and trees as cover as he circled the camp.

When he came level with the horse and cart, there was still no sign of anyone but the children, so he moved closer, keeping deep in the shadows.

The cart was roughly made, constructed with planks of wood that were barely sanded down. He hoped the dark stains he could see on the bottom were from water damage, not blood.

"You're big. That's unfortunate."

Theo turned quickly, lifting his sword as he spun.

The man who'd spoken flinched back at his speed, and they stared at each other as the fire crackled and the horse moved away a few steps, tail swishing.

The man hadn't been behind him moments before. Theo would have sworn it.

But he had heard there were spelled items, usually cloaks or pieces of clothing, that could hide a person—make them invisible.

He had walked past this man and not realized it.

The thought sat in his gut like rancid stew.

"You're fast. I didn't expect someone of your size to move so quickly." The man who spoke was thin and of medium height—old and white-haired. His eyes looked a little rheumy in the flickering light of the fire.

He was also unarmed.

"Why did you take my students?" Theo asked.

"Your students?" The man took a step back, and something in the movement told Theo he was injured. "That's interesting." He tilted his head to the side. "You also glow a little, like they do. I'm intrigued." The man turned his head, his hand going to a bag sitting on his hip, and as soon as he dropped his gaze, Theo moved, leaping forward, sword swinging, making sure to keep it turned so that he would hit this strange man with the flat of the blade, rather than its sharp edge.

He understood it would be better to have him for questioning than dead.

The man shied away, catching sight of the attack in his peripheral vision, and threw himself to the ground with a shriek.

"No!"

He threw what he'd drawn from his bag at Theo, and Theo felt the touch of something cold, that stung him where it touched his face and the hands he'd raised.

He brought the sword down, although the change in angle meant what he'd meant to be a broadside hit turned into a slice.

He heard the man screaming as the world spun around him and

he fell. As he hit the ground he realized he couldn't get air into his lungs.

He fought to suck in a breath, and the first trickle of air was like fire scorching his throat, it was so painful, but he pushed through to draw in more, aware he was lying helplessly on the ground, gasping like a fish out of water.

He caught movement, saw the man stagger to his feet, hand at his side, smeared in red. "You cut me. You cut me." He moved to the cart and came back, standing right beside Theo's head. "You're too big and dangerous for me to handle in your current form."

He leaned down and pushed something circular over Theo's head. He was breathing heavily, and this close, Theo could see he was gray-faced. Then the rope or whatever it was he'd pulled over Theo's head tightened around his neck, and his world went dark.

CHAPTER 3

MELODIE CLASPED her hands behind her and stretched, tipping back her head and arching her back.

She needed to walk around more throughout the day, to move instead of sitting still for so long, but she always got absorbed in her work and forgot the time.

She looked outside and realized it was at least mid-afternoon. The morning sun that came through her workshop window was long gone and the shadows were gathering.

She stepped closer and eyed her latest creation critically.

The ring looked good.

Exquisite, even.

It was a piece that their customer, Madam Renali, would be hard-pressed to find in Taunen, Grimwalt's capital, rather than lowly Illoa, on the outer edge of the country. And she would pay less for it here than if she'd commissioned it in Taunen.

Melodie didn't know what price Madam Renali had agreed with Vinest, but she knew she would only get a fraction of it.

She braced her hands on either side of the bench, and studied the piece carefully.

For her, the ring was lacking, but adding the final element was not something she could or would do for a paying customer in Vinest's shop.

Everything that she made straight—with just gold, silver and gems—seemed lacking these days.

She glanced at the ring on her own finger, which contained the little bit extra she had worked into it, and although it looked less expensive than the commissioned piece she'd just completed, it was worth far, far more, if anyone had known what it was.

She had been weighing the benefits and pitfalls of making these more enhanced pieces for a while.

It went against everything her father had taught her.

It would also mean she would have far more financial security than she currently had.

But financial security would mean nothing if she came to the wrong person's attention.

She hated having to weigh up her future financial stability with her own safety. And as she stared at the diamond ring she had just finished, she felt anger rising up inside her.

She had tried to bring up how little Vinest paid her with him in so many subtle ways. Round-about mentions of the pay of similar artisans; direct comparisons to other jewelers; everything she could think of.

It was time to be direct. Because she didn't like feeling this resentment, this fury at the end of a long day's work, rather than accomplishment for a job well done.

"Melodie. You finished?"

She turned with churning emotions at the sound of Vinest's voice.

She had lived with him since her father had died when she was sixteen. She was inclined to be loyal to him. But he seemed to think he needed to make her dependent on him to keep her.

She looked directly into his eyes. "I want a higher pay, Vinest."

He stopped short, squinting at her like she had squinted at her commission only moments before. "Where's this coming from? I pay you enough."

"No, you don't." She felt a rising pressure in her chest, and realized it was a feeling of betrayal.

It was probably her own fault. When her father had died, Vinest had taken her in, and she had seen him as a member of her family. His refusal to compensate her fairly hurt, because it felt as if her own uncle was cheating her. Except he wasn't her uncle.

It wasn't as if she had ever been a drag on his household. She had been useful to him since the day he'd given her the small room at the top of his house, in the eaves. And still, he wanted to squeeze every last drop out of her.

He looked at her warily, skirting around her to look at the ring still clamped in the holder on the bench. "It looks ready."

"It is." She drew in a breath. "You don't pay me enough to live on my own. I am a master jeweler and I cannot afford my own place to stay."

He turned to look at her, with a slightly surprised, mildly hurt look on his face, and she finally forced herself to admit it was false. He used it every time she tried to push back against him.

"You don't need a place to stay. You stay here."

She looked at him in silence for a long beat. Saw a faint glint of cunning in his eye. Then gave a sharp shake of her head.

This argument was over.

She would not convince him, and he would pretend that he was a kind and benevolent boss, because it was very much in his interests to keep her under his roof and working for apprentice wages.

It was time to make another plan.

She turned and headed for the door.

"Wait, where are you going?" He sounded a little sharp.

"Out," she said. "I need to stretch my legs. I've been sitting here all day."

"Bett has made pies for dinner," he said, a touch of relief in his voice. "Don't be late."

She looked at him in silence again, and then walked out, into the narrow passage that split the house between the business and their living quarters.

The door to the shop, which sat next to her studio, was closed, and she ignored it as she headed into the hall, lifting her bag from its hook by the door, and setting it across her chest.

She caught sight of herself in the mirror that hung to one side, and straightened her shirt and tucked stray strands of hair that had come undone from her braid behind her ears.

"Melodie."

She paused with the front door partly open and looked back down the dim passage, saw the hulking outline of Vinest standing by the shop door.

She waited.

"What made you bring the matter of money up now? I thought we were family."

She studied the dark outline of him, and the ring on her finger suddenly heated up.

She clenched her hand into a fist in surprise.

Then she turned thoughtfully away and stepped outside, stretching out her fingers and looking down at her middle finger as she headed for the town square.

The ring was a working of rose gold, which held what looked like a piece of rose quartz in the middle. It had the ability to sense danger and deception.

And Vinest had just lied.

He didn't see her as family at all.

CHAPTER 4

Melodie loved the market square.

It was surrounded on three sides by buildings, and the fourth side was open, a promenade along the river bank. Midway along the promenade was the bridge which joined the Grimwalt side to the Kassian side. It was wide enough to accommodate generous traffic in either direction, and there was a similar market square on the Kassian side, a mirror image to the one she stood in now.

Both sides were always busy, and there was a constant stream of bridge traffic, a consistent hum of voices and the clatter of hooves and cart wheels over cobbles. The traders liked to tease each other over which market was better, but the rivalry was friendly.

It hadn't always been this way.

Illoa used to be smaller.

Melodie had come through it as a child, although she barely remembered the village as it had been. When she and her father had returned when she was sixteen, he had commented often on how much it had grown since Kassia became Kassia and Cervantes, and formed a strong alliance with Grimwalt.

It was an interesting place to live—a border town that was a conduit for most of the trade between Kassia and Cervantes and Grimwalt, as well as Skäddar to the north.

It was easier for the Skäddar merchants to cut through Grimwalt than to go around through Jatan, and everyone benefited from the arrangement.

She certainly loved the ebb and flow of merchant caravans and lone traders that came through. They often set up stalls for a few days on either the Kassian or Grimwalt side of the bridge, bringing interesting items with them.

And sometimes they brought things she had spent her life pretending not to see.

The merchant carts usually set up around the square early in the day, and as it was late afternoon now, they were winding down. Some were closing up, some were content to sit and watch the sun set over the Malin River and wait for customers to wander by.

Hunger from a day spent bent over her work led Melodie straight to a food stall, where she threw caution—and the thought of supper—to the wind, and bought a funnel cake. She ate it slowly as she wandered past the stalls, enjoying the crispy crunch of the dough and the cool, cinnamon whipped cream in the center.

There were usually many months between her special finds, and she had last found something magically interesting only three weeks before, so she didn't expect much, but she liked to browse anyway, pausing at the overcrowded tables to look at the wares.

Her gaze passed with interest over carved wooden bowls, mosaic lamps and hand-dyed swatches of fabric, but nothing stood out to her.

When she turned down a new row of carts, though, she stopped dead, causing the person behind her to bump into her and swear softly. The jostling caused her to drop her cake, but she didn't even look down to where it fell.

She mumbled an apology without looking around, and the man swung past her, sending her an irritated look, but she could not take her eyes from the glow.

Good or bad, she wondered as she slowly walked toward it.

Sometimes it wasn't possible to tell, and she'd worked out over the years that most often the ones she couldn't read well were will-based spells, capable of being molded by the user.

She had seen plenty of magical items in her life. They winked and glimmered at her. Called to her.

Sometimes with a gentle gleam, occasionally with a more obvious glow. This one was as bright as she had ever seen.

The spell light came off the object in a wafting mist; golden and wispy. It swirled and eddied in the air, like the condensation off a massive block of ice set out on a sunny day.

She found it difficult to know where to direct her gaze when she reached the scruffy caravan halfway down the row, only tangentially taking note of its peeling paint and the chips gouged out of the intricate wooden carvings framing the window.

A table was set in front of the caravan's window and there was an awning, stretching from the edge of the roof, over the table, and held up by two poles which had been set inside two large pots filled with soil.

"Greetings." A small man with deep bags under his eyes and bushy gray eyebrows turned to her. He was busy packing some of his wares into a box on the ground. His gaze flicked from her to other passers-by, and she wondered why he seemed so nervous.

"May I have a quick look before you pack up?" Melodie tried to keep her voice even and her attention on the stallholder, instead of on the item on the table which was throwing off so much light.

"Most certainly." He straightened up and stepped back behind the table, waving a hand in invitation, and yet, she had a feeling he was anxious at her attention.

She squinted a bit as she leaned in.

The aura was coming from a slim, rectangular wooden box.

She wasn't surprised by the type of object. She had seen it all over the years. Boxes, scarves, mugs. She loved finding things she could work into her jewelry, like gems and beads, but those were rare.

"You're interested in the paints?" he asked.

"The paints?" She glanced at him, then back at the box. "What type of paints?"

"I'm not an artist," he said. "But I think you add water to them to use them. This isn't a new set and they are dried up to look at them now, but that is how they're supposed to be." He flipped the lid, and she saw the inside had eight small sections on the top and another eight on the bottom, with an open section running between them.

Each section contained a dried up cake of color and it looked as if someone had mixed some of the colors together in the middle, and hadn't washed it clean.

The glow didn't diminish when he opened the box, but it wasn't brighter, either.

"I make jewelry. This might be useful to me when I draw my designs." She said it as if to herself, thoughtfully. "What is the price?"

He gave her an amount and she stood, finger tapping her lips, considering it.

It was steep for a small wooden box of used watercolors. Absolutely a bargain for a spell-worked item of such strength.

She wondered if he knew what he had. She was so used to being the only one who could see spell work, she rarely considered it.

But the price tag . . .

And I still don't know what it does, she reminded herself. *Whether this is malicious magic or benign. Or if the magic will leave the good or the bad of it up to me.*

It didn't matter. She needed to have it. Needed to prevent someone who didn't know what it was harming themselves or others by using it.

"You drive a hard bargain," the old man said into the silence, the hint of worry she thought she'd detected in his eyes turning to quiet fear. He sent her a fake smile that showed a few gaps in his teeth. "How about a discount?"

She was surprised when he halved the amount. He must want to get rid of it, or he had been outrageously bold with the first offer.

His behavior made her wonder if he knew what he had, or whether he had come to own it through less than honest means and now wanted to get rid of it.

Whatever the reason, she couldn't leave it for sale.

"Done," she said, pulling her small coin purse from her shoulder bag and counting out the coins.

The stallholder took them in a way that reminded her of a magician's sleight of hand, delicately removing them from her palm with long, surprisingly slim fingers, and then they were gone.

He would make a good thief.

She picked up the box, felt the tingle against her skin, and slid it into her bag. The sudden dimming of light was a relief.

"Where did the paints come from?" she asked.

"I'm from Cattha," he said, although that didn't answer her question. "On my way to Taunen."

"Well, safe travels to you," she said, and turned away.

"You'll need to find some brushes," the man called from behind her. "I don't have any, but a few carts down, old Dame Carvaggo might have some."

"Thank you." She glanced back briefly, saw he had begun to pack up in earnest, and tried to remember if she had any brushes herself, but when she stopped at Dame Carvaggo, the lady was selling three for a single coin, so she bought them and turned toward the river and the bridge, drawn by the dance of afternoon light on the water.

She crossed the square and made her way to the promenade. There was no railing, just a straight drop down into the wide, slow waters of the Malin River, which meandered through the town— the border marker between Kassia and Cervantes and Grimwalt.

A goat bleated, and she turned to look.

It had bounded up from the lower bank at the side of the bridge, which, unlike where she stood, sloped down more gently to a narrow bar of sand rather than dropping straight into the water.

She stared. For a moment, she wondered if she had been so blinded by the box of paints earlier that she was mistaking the sunlight reflecting off the river for the brightness of the glow she could see around the goat's neck.

She watched as the goat moved closer to the pillar at the start of the bridge. It was tied to the bridge by a long coil of rope, but underneath that was something spell worked that was looped around the goat's neck—either a piece of string or twine.

If she thought the box of paints was bright with magic, the twine was a sun to the paintbox's moon. As she stared at it, it became a golden cage around the animal, and then it was a golden collar again.

The goat pawed at a scattering of offerings to Malin, the river spirit who kept the land fertile. There were flowers, the traditional wooden cups with Malin's face carved into them, and even a woven basket.

She had seen many things left in tribute over the years, but never a living creature.

As she stood there, staring, a woman walked over the bridge and placed an apple, another of the favored tributes to Malin, in front of the informal shrine.

"Don't eat this, creature," she said, pointing at the goat.

"If the goat is a tribute, then it doesn't matter if it eats the apple," Melodie said. "It's all tribute to Malin."

The woman turned to look at her, suspicious. "The goat is your tribute?"

Melodie wasn't a Grimwaldian native, and had never left a tribute to Malin. She shook her head.

"Someone's trying to have their goat fed for free," the woman said, looking at the goat with dislike. She bent down, picked the apple back up and threw it into the water.

The goat turned and ran down the bank, and when Melodie leaned over, she saw it standing on the thin edge of sand, looking at the apple as it swirled in the eddies and then was whisked off by the current.

When she turned back, the woman was walking away.

The goat came back up from the river and nosed through the

flowers and handmade gifts. Suddenly, it lifted its head and seemed to stare behind her.

She turned and saw it was the old man who'd sold her the paints. He had crossed the square and stood a little way back.

She brushed her hand over her bag. The chances of two things so saturated in powerful spell work being so close together at the same time defied coincidence.

"The goat is yours?" she asked as the old man eventually drew level with her.

He started, stared at her with surprise, then lifted both hands, waving them a little. The move seemed panicked. "No."

"But you put the goat here." She was only guessing.

He gave her such a shocked look, she knew she was right.

"You saw me?"

She said nothing, and he began to back away. "Take it. I only put it there because it's such a difficult animal."

"You're abandoning it?" Melodie crouched down and studied the twine, narrowing her eyes to see past the glow. It was dark copper, almost invisible against the goat's fur, and once again she saw the outline of a cage.

Within it was a man. Curled over. Trapped.

She nearly fell backward.

Just for a moment, she saw the shape of him; crouched, in agony.

Her gaze locked with the goat's—the man's—and as if he knew she had seen him, he walked toward her on four little goat legs.

She had only once before seen someone trapped in another shape by spell work. She had been seven, and just like now, it had been in a market square, although that time it had been even busier. It had been a bigger town and on market day, as well.

She had tried to explain what she was seeing to her father. That the bird in the cage at the back of a cart was a woman, not a canary. Tried to make him understand that she could see the woman in brief flashes, battering at the magic that held her.

He had taken some convincing, and when at last he understood, and they went back to find her, the cart was gone.

She had cried for a long time after that, and eventually her father had packed up and moved them away.

One of the many times he had done that.

She had felt the guilt of forcing them to move yet again, along with the agony of wondering if the woman had ever gotten free. The worry about it had never left her.

She would not let this end the same way.

The goat reached her and butted her knees with its head.

She crouched and curved a hand over its neck and turned to look up at the old man.

Something in her gaze must have alarmed him, because he took a quick step back.

"Whose goat is it, if not yours?" she asked.

He looked over at the line of stalls, then back to her and the goat. "Look, I found the goat a few days ago. I tried to look after it, but it's been nothing but trouble. I'm off to Taunen tomorrow morning, and I thought someone might take it if I left it by the bridge." The old man hunched his shoulders. "It'll have enough to eat from the tributes. Or children might feed it." He glanced down at the river. "There's plenty of water for it to drink."

"Found it, where?" she asked.

He paused, mouth working, and then he shook his head. "I can't remember." He glanced back at his stall again. "I've got to go."

"I thought you were only leaving for Taunen tomorrow morning," Melodie said.

He looked at her sharply, sucked in a breath. "I'm leaving tonight to get a little way out of town on the road to Taunen, so I can make an early start." He suddenly fumbled in his pocket, taking out the coins she'd paid him for the paints, and holding them out to her. "To feed the goat," he said.

She extended her hand and he dropped the coins onto her palm.

"You stole the paints, didn't you? And the goat." Whoever he had taken both things from was someone dangerous. He had two of the most powerful spell-worked items she'd ever seen. And he would be looking for them.

No wonder the trader was nervy.

He had to know he was being hunted.

The old man shook his head as he retreated. "No. I'm no thief."

Except everything in his demeanor told her he was.

He turned and hurried away, shuffling across the cobbles to his caravan.

While she had been talking to the woman about the goat, he'd put the table away and folded back the awning, and the caravan looked strangely naked and out of place among the other carts and stalls.

He moved to the pen of livestock to one side of the square, handed over a coin, and then led out a small donkey she assumed was his means of pulling the caravan.

The goat butted her knees again.

"I know, I know. We have to wait until he's gone. I don't want him to see me take you." She rose to her feet, her fingertips on the top of the goat's head.

Within minutes, the donkey was harnessed and the old man steered his caravan out of the square.

As soon as he turned down the main road out of town, she crouched again and began to work on the knot around the goat's neck, keeping her fingers away from the twine.

Sometimes when she touched something, she deactivated it. Not often, but enough to make her wary.

She didn't want a man with a rope around his neck to suddenly appear in the square.

No one was watching her that she could see. The sun was almost set, and where they were, crouched beside the bridge, was in a pool of shadow. But best to be cautious.

The rope was rough and hard to loosen, but she worked with her hands every day and her fingers were strong. After what felt like a lifetime, but was more likely ten minutes, she finally had it off.

The goat had stayed still while she worked, but the moment it was loose, it ran a few steps away from her.

She rose to her feet, arched her back, which was still stiff from a day spent bent over her workbench, and then looked over at the animal.

"I can get it off, but let's do it where no one is watching."

The goat studied her with golden eyes. Then it gave a little jump, as if in impatience.

"Let's go, then." She kept to the edge of the square, to where the shadows were longest.

Keeping hidden, keeping a low profile. Everything her father ever taught her.

He had died sticking to that philosophy.

She wouldn't abandon it now.

She headed home, taking the smaller streets, thinking through her options. The goat trotted docilely along by her side.

Vinest wasn't safe. Her ring had told her that.

She had seen the protection spell on it when she'd found it at the market months ago, but she hadn't known whether it was a general protection, or something more specific.

After what happened this afternoon, she now knew it was very specific.

Vinest was angry enough with her to do her physical harm.

The thought of how her ring had heated, the knowing she'd had in that moment that he wished to strike her for her lack of acquiescence, made her turn one street away from home and head for the smithy.

Jackson would be done for the night and down at the inn, drinking and eating his dinner.

She reached the double doors, bent, and felt between the stones that edged a small flower bed, pulling out the spare key.

She wondered if Jackson even remembered it was there.

She unlocked the door, opened it just enough for her and the goat to squeeze through, and stepped into the dark, warm forge.

The smell of hot iron and smoke lingered in the air, and the furnace threw out a red glow.

She didn't bother to light a lamp, she used the firelight to walk to the bench of tools, found a sharp pair of pliers, and sat down on one of the sawn-off logs Jackson used as chairs in a place where tiny sparks flew around and burned whatever they touched.

"Come here, I'll cut it off."

The goat approached warily, as if suddenly worried about her intentions.

She said nothing, sitting patiently, and with a sudden sigh, it pushed up against her, laying its head on her lap.

She took the pliers, slid them between the fur and the twine, and cut.

<h1 style="text-align:center">CHAPTER 5</h1>

HE WAS FREE.

Theo tried to rise from his crouch in front of the woman and cramps gripped him. He toppled to the side, unable to straighten up, the pain intense.

The woman reached out to catch him as he fell, lunging forward, but he was head and shoulders taller than her and considerably heavier, although she did manage to cushion his fall a little.

He gritted his teeth to stop himself groaning.

He didn't try to get up. He lay, curled on his side until the pain faded, then turned on his back and slowly stretched out his limbs, feeling the muscles in his back sing with relief as he was at last able to stretch out.

He turned his head to look at the woman.

She had landed on the floor beside him and was leaning against the leg of a workbench, knees bent, arms looped around her shins.

Her hair was long and the color of chocolate, dark and heavy. At her hairline, around her face, some strands were golden, and here and there, caught in the light from the forge, they gleamed as if she'd threaded golden silk through her braid.

She was beautiful. And somehow, she had saved him.

Theo closed his eyes, then opened them again slowly, just to confirm he was himself again.

The light was low, but the woman was clear enough, her chin resting on top of her knees, her gaze fixed on him. The copper twine that had imprisoned him was hanging from one of her fingers.

From his place on the floor he held out his hand, and as if she immediately understood what he meant, she dropped the twine into his palm without a word. He slowly rolled to his feet, stretching again, and felt the bones in his spine pop. He limped to the furnace and threw the twine into it, and it flared green before it melted.

Now he was properly free.

He looked back at her.

She remained on the floor, eyes on the flames, a serene look on her face, as if he had freed her, as well.

"Who are you?" he asked. He hardly recognized his voice, it was so rough.

"Oh." She looked up at him and gave a shy smile. "I'm Melodie."

He offered her a hand and she took it, her eyes widening a little as he lifted her effortlessly to her feet.

Her hand felt calloused, and she had a firm grip.

"I'm Theo. I owe you."

She studied him, shook her head. "You don't owe me for doing the right thing."

"How did you know I was in there?" No one else had. He had been tied to that pole for a night and almost a full day, and all anyone had seen was a goat.

He had only known that was what he'd been turned into because he'd seen his reflection in the sluggish waters of the Malin River.

The panic of his first moments, realizing he was a different shape, that he had a rope around his neck, that he was mute and powerless, would haunt him forever.

She hesitated. "I don't usually talk about it."

"You could see me?" He thought about it. "Could you only see the magic, or could you see me, the man?"

She looked at him for so long in silence, he thought she wasn't going to answer. Then she gave a tiny shake of her head. "The twine was bright with spell work. That's all I saw, at first. When I got close enough, I saw you once. The magic of the spell woven into the copper twine was fighting to keep you hidden in a cage."

"You knew it was the twine keeping me trapped?" He hadn't even noticed the twine in the beginning.

She nodded.

"How?" As he asked the question, he saw her withdraw. She physically made herself smaller, tucking her arms in close to her body and dipping her head.

"Hey." He reached out a hand, slid his fingers against the smooth skin of her chin and tilted her face back up to his. "You never have anything to fear of me. Ever."

She studied him, eyes that were a fascinating mix of dark blue and green assessing him for a long moment.

"My father died keeping what I do secret," she said. "I have never discussed it, especially since I saw him killed on the street, and if ever I am tempted, I remember that he sacrificed his very life to keep me invisible and safe."

"I don't want you to break any personal vows," he said. "I'm just trying to understand what happened to me."

She stepped back, then let out a sigh. "Can I just tell you that I could see the twine held a spell, and when I got closer, I could see that it held you trapped."

"Yes."

She could see spells. That was extraordinary. Theo suddenly understood why her father had worried about others knowing her power.

The rulers of Kassia and Cervantes would be delighted to have her on their staff. But other, less principled rulers, might not be so pleasant to work for.

"And I'm in Illoa?" He guessed it because of the dual towns on either side of the river, and it was the direction he'd been headed as he chased down the abductor.

She nodded. "On the Grimwalt side."

"Who was the old man who tied me to the bridge?"

Melodie shook her head. "A trader. He claimed he found you. He said he was headed for Taunen."

"He knew you were going to free me." Theo was sure of it. She had hardly been subtle.

Melodie shrugged. "Maybe."

"If he meets up again with the man who put that spell around my neck, he might tell him about you." Theo didn't want this woman in his abductor's sights. And whatever the connection between the two men, the one who'd taken the children was not to be underestimated.

"My guess is the trader will try as much as possible to avoid meeting that man again." Melodie paused. "Of course, someone with access to the kind of spell work involved might be difficult to shake."

"Why is he going to try to avoid him?" Theo thought back to what had happened, but he couldn't remember much at all. When he had come back to himself, he had been too busy reacting to the horror of his circumstances.

"He stole something from the spell worker who enchanted you. He stole you, too, is my guess. And then had second thoughts. My guess is he probably deeply regrets ever crossing paths with the spell worker in the first place." Melodie slid a stray lock of hair behind her ear.

"How do you know this?" Theo realized he needed to sit, that his legs were not quite steady, and he found a seat on one of the thick, round logs that were placed around the forge.

"I bought the item he stole," Melodie said. "The spell worked into it is so strong, I couldn't let it carry on in the world unsupervised."

"You have it now?" Nothing from the man who'd taken the children would be useful or good.

Melodie turned and picked up the square bag she'd been carrying. She took out a small, slim box.

He studied it. "What is it?"

"A wooden watercolor paint box." She opened it, and he could see the little holders of color along the top and bottom, with a place to mix colors in the middle.

"That is magical?" He couldn't see anything special about it.

"Very magical. The only thing I've ever seen with more magic is the copper twine around your neck." She hesitated. "And something else, long ago, when I was little. But that was destroyed."

"Are you going to throw it in the furnace?" He couldn't see the sense in keeping it.

She hesitated. "I would like to work out what it can do, first. In case I see something like it again. And it may be useful."

"It's from *him*," he said. "How could it be useful?"

"It may have been in his possession, but that doesn't mean he made it. The copper twine was very different. It was right that you threw it into the fire. This . . ." She snapped it closed. "This isn't the same."

He understood he was reacting on instinct. On his utter hatred for the man, but he couldn't see why she would take the chance.

She studied him as she put the box back into her bag. "I've had to watch too many people in pain, in fear, or danger from spell work. If I can use my knowledge to change things for them, it helps me make peace with all the times my father refused to allow me to intervene when I was a child. I never destroy anything unless I can plainly see its only function is evil."

"And have you saved anyone?" he asked, aware there was a challenge in his voice.

"Other than you?" She tipped her head so she could look him in the eye and he winced. "I have."

Fair enough. "How much do you think the trader who tied me to the bridge knows about the man who enspelled me?"

She tilted her head. "I think he knew a lot more than he was saying. But he lied about it. He wouldn't explain anything to me."

Fury suddenly leaped inside him, and Theo grimaced. "He'll say something to me."

She blinked at him, eyes wide, and he cleared his throat.

"We need to chase him down and find out what he does know."

"We?" She looked at him with interest.

He hadn't realized until this moment, but he still needed her. This was a case steeped in spell work, and he would be foolish indeed not to ask for help from someone who could see spell work.

He gave a slow nod. "I need to go across the bridge to the Kassia and Cervantes military barracks for supplies and a new mount, and, if you are available, I would like to hire your services," he said.

She did not look as if she hated the idea, he saw with relief.

"My services?"

"You can see spell work. I cannot. I am after someone who uses spell work as a weapon." He lifted his hands. "I believe you will be invaluable."

She continued to look at him. "How would that work?"

"You are an expert in spell work?" He asked it as a question but he knew he was stating a fact.

She gave a reluctant nod.

"So the Crown would pay you an expert's wage." He named the amount.

She went still. "The Crown?"

"I am a lieutenant for the kingdom of Kassia and Cervantes."

She studied him, for the first time looking at what he wore. As a resident of Illoa she would have seen his uniform before, he hoped. After a long moment she nodded her head. "It will be dangerous. Why are you going after him? Why not just leave?"

"Because I was chasing after him before he enspelled me. I'm not the only person he took," Theo told her. "He kidnapped four of my students. They are only thirteen years old."

"He transformed them, too?" She looked deeply shocked.

Theo shook his head. "No, he somehow put them into a deep

sleep. When I last saw them, they were trussed up and unable to move."

"You teach youngsters to be soldiers?" she asked.

"I do two weeks of training of young Cervantes recruits, just like every senior officer. We rotate the duty."

"And he has four of them?"

Theo nodded.

"And you will pay me fairly." She didn't ask it as a question, but stated it as a fact.

He nodded anyway. He had already given her the terms, and she must deem them to be fair.

She held out her hand to shake. "You have a deal."

CHAPTER 6

"You need to rest," Melodie said.

She'd noticed how he'd collapsed onto the log near the furnace, and she had seen the pain on his face as she'd freed him.

It was a handsome face, with straight, dark brows and sharp cheekbones.

He was a little intimidating, as well, but when he'd promised she would never have anything to fear of him, she had believed him. And her ring had not so much as twinged.

"Unfortunately, you're right." He rose to his feet, and she thought she saw a tiny wince as he reached his full height.

She was tall, but he was much taller—a true Cervantes warrior from what she'd observed of the breed when they came through Illoa on diplomatic trips.

Both the men and the women were tall and muscular, their hair dark, their eyes light. From what she could see, he was not lying about his rank or affiliation.

She had seen uniforms like the one he wore many times.

The Cervantes hadn't worn uniforms for a long time, but slowly, after they'd defeated Kassia and as Kassia and Cervantes became a united kingdom, they had begun to see the value in representing the country, even if it was a more informal uniform than many other armies.

The trousers were usually black, but sometimes dark gray. The shirt beneath their dark jackets, which were cut a specific way to enable easy sword work and archery, was the most prized item by the soldiers. They were said to be embroidered by the queen herself.

Melodie had long known that each one was spelled with protection. Which meant either the queen of Kassia and Cervantes was a spell worker, or she employed one to protect her troops.

Suddenly realizing the import of that, she fixed her gaze on the pale gray collar of his shirt, visible beneath his jacket. "Is that your shirt from the queen?" she asked.

He frowned, momentarily confused by her question. "No. We only each get one, and I left it behind on this trip."

She gave a nod, and wondered if the shirt would have protected him against a spell, or whether it was more calibrated to arrows, swords and knives.

"Is it common knowledge our queen gives us a shirt she has personally embroidered?" Theo asked.

Melodie nodded. She could see he looked unhappy about that, but there was nothing to be done about it.

"I cannot offer you a place to sleep," she said, and realized how upset the thought made her. She could only imagine the reaction from Vinest if she were to bring a Cervantes warrior to the door. "I might not have a place myself, if I make it known I am leaving with you."

He paused, glancing toward the door that clearly led out of the forge into the house beside it.

She shook her head. "Not there. My father worked here before he died, and I spent a year living here, which is why I knew where to find the key. I live a few streets over now." She led the way out, and locked up behind them.

"I'll go over to the Kassia and Cervantes side of the town," he said. "There's a barracks there and they'll give me everything I need."

That was a relief. She gave a nod. "When do you expect we will leave?"

"Early tomorrow morning." There was a leashed violence in him, as if he were still straining against the magical cage that had bound him. "I will be rested enough by then."

That was good. Better than waiting, while Vinest tried whatever it was he would surely try to keep her.

"What's worrying you?" He slowed as they approached her house, and she realized her steps had shortened and her every move was signaling her reluctance to face Vinest. "What I'm asking you to do is dangerous, but I swear, I will keep you as safe as I can."

She tilted her head to look up at him. She had gone against many spell workers before, usually hiding what she was doing. She knew it was never safe. "I believe you."

It was Vinest she worried about. That flare of danger from him that her ring had warned her of.

If anything would set off violence in him, it would be understanding he was losing her.

And she couldn't even tell the truth about why she had been hired. She would rather not say anything at all.

"Good." He glanced up at the house as she came to a stop by the front door. "This is it?"

She nodded. "You will have to provide me with a horse. I don't have one of my own."

He inclined his head. "That can be arranged. Pack light, but don't worry about food. I'll get supplies at the barracks."

That was good, because Betts would not allow her to take anything from the kitchen. The housekeeper hoarded food as if it were part of the gems and precious metals in Vinest's safe.

Theo reached out and gently grasped her upper arms. "You saved me, and I cannot say how grateful I am." He couldn't stop the sudden shudder that gripped him, and she saw the horror at what had happened to him etched on his face for a moment before he managed to soften his features. "I'm also grateful you've agreed to assist me. Thank you."

He was still holding her, so she lifted her hands and rested them on his biceps, aware of the intimacy of the pose. "I am glad I could help you, and I just today decided to leave my job, so your offer is quite serendipitous."

Light blossomed from upstairs, spilling out of the parlor window, and she could see from the light that filtered down on them that his features were strained with fatigue.

"Go rest," she told him, aware that Vinest was most likely looking down at her.

Her lieutenant must have been aware as well, although how, she didn't know, and he looked up at the window. "You'll be all right?"

She nodded, aware of the craziness that for the first time since she'd come to live with Vinest, she didn't actually know if that were true. "I'll see you tomorrow morning."

"'Til tomorrow." He turned and walked away, his stride easy and quick, despite the exhaustion that was dragging him down.

He headed toward the bridge, to cross to the Kassia and Cervantes side, and she headed for the door.

To the house she used to think of as home.

CHAPTER 7

SHE STEPPED INTO THE HOUSE, the scent of chicken pie wafting from the kitchen in the back.

She hung up her coat but kept her bag with her. She would need it to pack some of her things.

"Dinner is over." Betts met her in the narrow passage behind the stairs.

"That's fine. I'll take something up to my room." Melodie didn't like Betts, and Betts didn't like her.

It was a circular problem.

She would have embraced Betts as a friend, as family, but had always been met with sulkiness and annoyance. She had finally worked out that Betts didn't like her because she saw Melodie as an impediment to getting Vinest to marry her.

It was a pity it had to be that way, but now, it didn't matter. She was leaving, and the thought of that, from the moment Theo had offered her a job, caused such a massive weight to lift off her, she couldn't believe she hadn't noticed she was carrying it before now.

"No." Betts blocked her way. "*I* control the kitchen. *I* say if you can't be bothered to show up on time, you don't get to eat."

Melodie studied Betts with interest. Her face was flushed with anger and her hands were balled into fists.

Then she shrugged, turned, and walked away, back to the stairs. She would pack now. Leave now. The thought almost made her giddy.

Perhaps Theo would find a place for her at the barracks, or she could spend a night at the inn on the Kassia and Cervantes side of Illoa.

"Where are you going?" Betts was coming after her, hands still clenched at her side.

"What does it matter to you?" Melodie paused on the second step up to her room. "I'm not eating your food, so you shouldn't care, either way."

"What's this about not eating?" Vinest stood at the top of the stairs.

"She doesn't get food if she can't be here on time. You said." Betts looked up at him, mouth a tight line.

"Oh, Betts was most definitely following your orders." Melodie gave a nod. The open hostility was new, but obviously Vinest had emboldened her.

"I was joking," Vinest said. He looked past her down to Betts, and gave a tiny shake of his head.

Melodie's ring warmed on her finger, and she looked up at him with a cheerful smile.

Liar.

"Well, Betts seems very set on my not getting any of her food, so I'll go out for some." She continued up the stairs, wondering if Vinest was going to move out of the way.

A tickle of fear snaked down her spine, because he could easily push her from where he stood. And he wanted to hurt her. Her ring told her as much.

But she would be no good to him, crumpled at the bottom of the steps.

"It's not her food." Vinest snapped the words, his look at Betts suddenly furious. "I say who gets it and who doesn't."

"And you said she doesn't." Betts wasn't going to let it go. Vinest had tried to make her look petty and foolish, and she was refusing to play along.

"The food at the square smelled delicious. I just came from there. I'll have a night out." Melodie angled to the left, where Vinest had left a little space, but as she reached the top, sliding past him, his hand shot out and gripped her arm.

She thought of how Theo had held her in the same spot only minutes before, and the difference between them.

"A night out?" he said.

"After all, that piece I finished for Madam Renali took a lot out of me. It'll fetch a very handsome fee. Enough for Betts to cook up a storm. Because I certainly won't be getting much of a share of the payment, will I?" She glanced down the stairs, and Betts drew her lips back to show her teeth at the reminder of who made the money in this household.

"Who was the man?" Vinest asked. "The one who walked you home?"

"A friend of mine." Melodie said.

"I didn't know you had such . . . friends." Vinest hesitated over the word.

She shrugged. "I'm twenty-two. Why wouldn't I?"

"He looked like he was in uniform." Vinest didn't like the soldiers who came and went through town. She had always wondered why.

They didn't buy jewelry, which was a mark against them from a jeweler's perspective, but that was the only thing she could think of that wouldn't be to his liking.

"He's a lieutenant for the Crown of Kassia and Cervantes," she said, and Vinest's grip on her arm tightened enough to make her wince.

She tried to tug her arm away and he looked down as if he had forgotten he had a hold of her.

"I don't like soldiers."

She shrugged again. She could do nothing about his likes and dislikes.

"Is this revenge? Some petty game because you think I underpay you?" he asked.

"Revenge?" she drew back, eyebrows raised. "I went for a walk, met a friend, and walked back. What part of that is a game?" She looked him in the eye. "And I don't think you underpay me. I know."

"You will not go out." His face had gone frighteningly blank, and she had to draw on all the courage in her to keep her face unmoved.

"Am I a prisoner here, Vinest?"

He finally released her arm. "No, of course not. I didn't mean you can't spend your free time as you will, but Betts made dinner and you disrespected her by not coming in in time."

"I want more pay, so I can move out and get my own place." She smiled at him. "I'm sure Betts would be as happy with that solution as I would."

"Is this . . . friend of yours responsible for this new foolishness?" Vinest's eyes narrowed.

There was no sense talking about this anymore. Nothing she said would make any difference, and she didn't plan to stay anyway. Trying to negotiate more pay was a moot point, as was the squabble about food.

"No." She moved past him and went to her room. She turned back to look at him from the doorway. "I'll see you tomorrow."

"What about dinner?" he said. "I don't want you going hungry. As you said, you worked hard today."

"I told you, I'll freshen up and then go back to the square and get some dinner from the stalls."

"Nonsense. Betts has made a wonderful pie. No sense spending good money on food when we have plenty here."

She extended both hands, palms up. "You refuse to let me eat, you order me to eat. Which is it?" she asked him softly, lifting one hand and then the other.

"I was angry you didn't come home, especially after our . . . words earlier." Vinest tried to look calm and fatherly. He was not succeeding, but she didn't think he realized that. "I don't want you to go out in the dark, and feel as if you aren't welcome in your own home."

"I don't feel welcome here, and you've made it clear it isn't my own home, or I wouldn't have to account for my every movement." She stepped into her room. "We can talk about this later, Vinest. I'm tired and I'm hungry and I don't feel like arguing with either of you."

She closed her door, and not for the first time wished she had a key to lock it behind her. Vinest had claimed it was lost, and when she'd asked for a new one to be made, he had looked sadly at her and asked if she didn't trust him and Betts to keep her privacy.

She moved quickly, choosing sturdy trousers and shirts, plenty of socks and a few knitted tunics to wear under her coat.

She thought she heard someone outside her door and stopped, turning to see if Vinest would knock.

Instead, she heard the distinct click of a key turning in the lock.

CHAPTER 8

The home Melodie thought she'd had for the last six years was all an illusion.

She had been too traumatized and young to notice anything off when she'd first moved in, and she'd been grateful to Vinest and happy to follow his wishes.

She'd enjoyed learning to be a gold and silversmith, using the skills her metalsmith father had taught her, but on a more delicate scale.

It was only now that she chose not to accept Vinest's rules that she saw the conditionality of their relationship.

Her father would be devastated that the friend he trusted would treat her this way.

And she had no way out.

No obvious way out, anyway.

She was on the second floor, and there was no convenient tree or roof top for her to shimmy down near her window. It was a straight drop down to the paved back yard.

She stood at the window and looked down anyway, mulling over her options.

She could wait until morning, when Theo would arrive to fetch her. She had no doubt he would not go away quietly if Vinest hadn't let her out by then. But she didn't want the ugliness of that, and she didn't want Vinest to win.

She pulled out the box she kept her design sketches in, taking them out and stacking them in a neat pile, and then lifted the false bottom up.

She had bought this box at the market, because she knew that her room had been searched more than once. She thought it was Betts, looking for something to chastise her about, but now she wondered if it was Vinest.

It didn't matter. Neither of them had found what she didn't want found, which was her collection of magical items. She set them out on the bed.

She had destroyed way more than she'd kept, and she had anonymously gifted others to those who needed them. Besides the ring she wore on her finger, there was a blackened silver brooch, which had magic too faint to work out. She had thought she would smelt it and fashion it into a new piece when she understood exactly what it did.

Then there was a remedies book that fell open to the correct recipe for whatever illness you spoke. She had found it three weeks ago, and she planned to give it to the right person, but that kind of obvious magic made many uncomfortable, and she had yet to pass it on.

The final item was a handkerchief. It had a tiny, beautifully made embroidery on the corner, and it reminded her of someone she'd once known.

It protected a specific wearer, not anyone else, and she only kept it because it was no use to anyone, and the feeling of it when she touched it reminded her of a time when her father was alive, and they were not so alone.

It wasn't much—she didn't like keeping anything she wasn't going to use—and they fit easily into her bag. Only the paints were left.

She sat down at her desk and touched the box with her fingertips.

It was so spell infused, her fingers tingled at the contact.

She opened the box, studied the colors.

She was proficient at drawing—she had learned from her father to always draw before she made anything—but the more she stared at the inside of the box, the heavier the weight of possibilities seemed to grow.

If she drew something with these paints, it would be significant.

She had seen many types of spell work. The golden light of a spell-worked rope that fed from its victim's energy. The twine around Theo's neck that acted like a cage. The bead in the center of her ring that felt protective to her, but this . . . this felt like she could draw something and bring it into being.

She had no fresh paper—it was all downstairs in her workshop—but the pile of her old designs sat near her elbow, so she flipped them over. She took out the brushes she'd bought in the market, poured a little water from the jug on her nightstand into a bowl, and thought of something simple.

She drew a key on the back of a used sheet of parchment.

It wasn't in her to do a sloppy job, so she took some care in crafting it.

When she was done, she sat back and watched it dry, and the moment it did, the paper turned blank, with a real key weighing it down.

She touched it much like she'd touched the box earlier. Gingerly, with her fingertips.

It felt cool and solid.

She picked it up and walked to the door. Hesitated, and then thrust it into the lock.

It didn't fit.

She withdrew it, tried again. But it wasn't going to open the door for her.

So this magic was specific.

She had come across few items in her time that weren't.

Protection as a spell was usually as broad as it got, and even then, she got the sense of armor over the person, not a general protection against everything.

So what, specifically, could she draw?

She looked at the hinges on the door, thought about drawing some kind of lever. But it wouldn't be a silent effort, and it would bring both Betts and Vinest running.

She would rather leave quietly and without their knowledge, and if it wasn't going to be through the door, then it would have to be out the window.

She walked over to it, studied the drop.

She needed rope.

She returned to the desk and looked down at the paper that had produced the key. Would using the same sheet again work?

She drew a coil of rope, using the color there was the most of—orange. She considered drawing it like the key, from a bird's eye view, but she usually drafted her jewelry designs as three dimensional images, and she experimented with drawing the rope the same way—a coiled pile of it.

It took longer to dry than the key, and it might not work, but in case it did, she got up and looked for something to tie it to.

She settled on the leg of her bed, which was close to the window, and when she turned around, the image was still on the paper.

The paint was dry, it just hadn't worked.

Sighing, she took another piece of paper and drew rope from the center of the page, turning it as close on itself as she could. With its capacity to hold her weight in mind, she made it as wide as she could, as narrow as she dared.

When she was done, she put the page carefully aside and quickly started a new one.

She would need a few pages to draw the length of rope she needed.

When she was done with the second page, the first had dried, and the rope had shimmered into being.

She tested it, and it seemed to hold strong. She tied knots into it at various intervals, because she would need them to help her down.

After she tied one end to the bed, she fed it out the window and saw it fell about a quarter of the way.

As she turned back to her desk, she saw the rope lying on top of the page disappear, and with a sound of disbelief, turned to look at the rope she'd tied around her bed.

It was gone, too. And so was the key, now she was looking for it.

She closed her eyes, feeling a hard, tight sense of hopelessness.

Then anger replaced it.

She would not give up.

She thought back to how long she'd been fussing around with the rope before it disappeared. At least ten minutes.

She understood there was a time limit now, and she knew she had to move quickly.

She lined two pages up, got everything ready, and began to draw as fast as she could, fitting as much rope onto each page as possible.

As soon as the first page dried, she tied the rope to the leg of her bed, rushed back and tied the second rope to it.

She shoved the blank pages into her bag, along with the box of paints, the small bowl and the brushes, went to the window and tossed the rope down.

It didn't reach all the way to the ground, but it was close enough. She could free fall for the last bit.

She had only opened the window a little way to throw the rope down, but she needed it wide open to get herself and her things out. It stuck, and she pushed it. Hard.

It opened on a shriek loud enough to wake the dead.

She didn't have time to worry or retreat, she scrambled over the window sill, grabbed the rope, and set her feet on the wall, then began walking down the side of the house.

"Melodie."

The voice sounded so close, she almost let go of the rope.

She glanced quickly across—all she had time for—and saw Vinest staring at her from his own open window.

She didn't respond, just kept going down.

"Melodie, you're going to kill yourself."

She decided that keeping him talking meant he wasn't racing to her room, trying to pull her back up.

She could slide down and talk at the same time.

"This is on you, Vinest." Her foot slipped on the moss that grew on the side of the house, and with a jerk, she was suddenly dangling from the rope. Her arms took the strain, and she scrabbled her feet, and finally found purchase.

She didn't have long. She was sure of it, so she began moving even faster.

"You nearly fell there. And you say I'm making you climb down the side of the house?" Vinest had gone silent when she'd slipped, and now his hiss of outrage was itself enraging.

She looked up again, saw he was leaning as far out of his window as he could. "You locked me in my room. Like a prisoner. Shame on you, Vinest. My father would be devastated."

That remark hit hard. She saw him flinch back.

"You were trying to leave me. To break free," he said, waving the hand that wasn't clutching the window sill.

"So? Again, only prisoners need to break free."

"I need you. Your designs are the signature of the business."

She knew it, but he had never admitted that to her before.

"If you'd paid me fairly and given me my independence, I would have kept working for you," she told him. "Now, no matter what, your behavior tonight is the end of things."

She was nearly at the bottom, and suddenly the rope disappeared. She cried out as she fell, stumbling and then landing hard on her side on the slate paving stones that covered the back courtyard.

She looked up, felt the hot prickle of fear down her arms as she saw the extent of the drop, and got to her feet.

At the sight of her standing on the ground below, Vinest suddenly seemed to realize she was out of his reach.

"Stop. I'm sorry I locked you in. It was a poor decision." His voice was wheedling.

The kitchen door banged open, and Melodie turned to see Betts, wearing a dressing gown and a scarf on her head.

She stayed in the doorway, arms crossed over her chest, mouth a thin line. "How did you get down?"

Melodie couldn't help the laugh that exploded out of her. "Interesting question."

"Well, get off with you, if you're going." Betts half-turned back into the kitchen, dismissing her.

"Goodbye, Betts." There was truly nothing else she could say. It was sad, but it wasn't on her. She turned for the back gate, hitching her satchel across her chest.

"Wait a minute. What are you taking with you?" Betts called after her, voice harsh.

Melodie glanced over her shoulder, and another laugh of disbelief escaped her throat. "You've searched my room often enough, I'm sure you have a good idea." Melodie opened the back gate, stepped into the alley that ran behind the house, and pushed it shut behind her.

She heard Vinest raise his voice, shouting at Betts to stop her, but Betts wasn't so inclined.

The sound of their argument faded as she increased her pace. She reached the road and crossed another two parallel streets before she turned toward the bridge.

Vinest would not simply let her go.

He was probably throwing on clothes right now, and he'd go to the bridge to stop her. He suspected Theo was her inspiration for leaving, and the Kassia and Cervantes soldiers barracked on their own side of the river.

He might go to Jackson first, though, and check the forge just in case she was merely changing residences and had decided to move to the smithy for a while. But in the event he went to the bridge first, she began to jog.

The square and the streets around the river were swirling with fog when she reached them. And she decided that was a good thing for her.

She stumbled a few times before she got to the bridge itself, but no one tried to stop her, and there was no sign of Vinest.

There used to be guard gates at both ends of the bridge, but that had fallen away as the compact between Kassia and Cervantes and Grimwalt settled into a long-term alliance.

Now there was a booth at the midway point of the bridge, to record the names of those who came across.

She reached the sentries, one for each country, and gave her name, looking back toward the square, although it was almost impossible to see anything but the swirling white of the fog.

"Someone chasing you?" The Kassian and Cervantes soldier asked her, perking up from his sleepy slump.

She glanced at him. "Maybe."

The Grimwaldian soldier came a bit more to attention, too. "Who?"

"My former boss." She turned to the Kassia and Cervantes soldier. "Do you know the lieutenant who came over the bridge earlier?"

He gave a slow nod.

"Did he go to the barracks?" she asked.

"Yes."

"All done." The Grimwaldian said, lifting his pen with a flourish.

"Thank you." She set off at a jog, with a last look over her shoulder.

"Melodie!" Vinest seemed to burst out of the fog.

"Keep going. We'll sort it for you." The Kassia and Cervantes soldier murmured to her.

She ran.

Behind her, she heard the Grimwaldian soldier stop Vinest.

"Sir, you have to give your name."

"Melodie, I won't do it again. I swear. Just come back."

"And what is it that you did?" one of the soldiers asked, a sudden chill in his voice, and then the fog swallowed them, and she reached the end of the bridge.

It felt like reaching freedom.

CHAPTER 9

THEO HAD BEEN EXHAUSTED EARLIER, but after getting across the bridge, finding the barracks, and eating a meal, he'd found a second wind.

Captain Draper had hauled him into her office straight after he'd pushed away from the mess hall table, and he'd decided to tell her the whole story.

He needed assistance, and while he wanted to keep the kidnapping as quiet as possible, he also didn't want to lie.

The only part he held back was the exact nature of Melodie's skills.

"You trust her?" Ellen Draper asked. "The woman you want to include in the rescue?"

"She didn't hesitate to free me from the spell I was under. She did nothing but help me. She'll be useful when we catch up to the bastard who took the kids." He laid out his reasoning simply, ticking them off on his fingers.

"And she says the merchant who took you from your abductor might know where he went?"

"She thinks he knows more than he is prepared to admit. And right now, he's our best lead." Theo hoped she was right, because otherwise, they were just stumbling around the vast forests of Grimwalt with no direction.

Draper gave a slow nod. "All right. I'll approve the expenses for her. You say the general has gone back to Ta-lin to raise the alarm?"

"Yes. The commander and the queen are in residence there. That's why the princess was allowed to come on the training run."

"Shit." Draper shook her head. "What a mess."

"My uncle took it very badly," Theo said. "It brought back too many memories. I was worried about leaving him."

"I'll send four of my people down to Ta-lin at first light." Draper wrote something on the parchment in front of her. "I've got roughly half Cervantes and half Kassian soldiers stationed here. I'll make sure two of the group who ride down are Cervantes. Best case, if they meet the rescue party coming the other way, they'll be recognized. If they find the general is having trouble on the journey to Ta-lin because of remembered trauma of the Chosen Camps, they will help him to continue on his way, and it will still be better if some of them are Cervantes."

Theo gave a nod of approval. "Please tell whoever goes down to Ta-lin to keep this extremely quiet." Theo leaned back in his chair. "How many can you spare for me?"

"I want to give you my whole cohort," she said. "I really want to come along."

There was silence between them for a beat, because Theo knew she meant every word.

"But realistically?" he asked.

She sighed. "Realistically I can give you four, which means we are down to half our number. My standing orders are never to go below that amount." She pulled a fresh sheet of paper towards her. "It isn't as important, but I'll give you two Cervantes, two Kassians in your group, too."

"I think a small, tight group will be better than a large one, anyway." Theo tapped the edge of Draper's desk with his fingers. "Can you give me your best?"

"I can." She scratched her quill over the page.

"Don't tell them what it's for." Theo leaned forward. "I'll tell them as soon as we're out of Illoa. I don't want this leaking."

She gave a nod.

"And I'd like you to tie a goat up at the bridge and set someone in the square to watch who pays it any attention. If me and my team miss the trader, or if Melodie is wrong about the trader knowing more than he says, the abductor may come back looking for what he thinks is me. If he does, it's another lead back to the children."

She sat straighter, as if she hadn't considered that. "That's an excellent idea." She blew out a breath. "To be honest, it feels like it's a necessity and I won't simply be waiting here, stuck by my orders."

"It is a necessity."

"What type of goat?" Draper asked.

He tried to remember what he'd looked like in that form, but he'd only caught glimpses of himself in the reflection on the water, and he was so preoccupied with the horror of the spell that trapped him, he hadn't paid attention. "Maybe Melodie could tell us," he said. "When I bring her back here tomorrow morning, remind me to ask her."

Draper stood. "I'll organize everything you need. You look—" she paused, considering her words.

"Like I was a goat for three days?" Theo asked, a tiny smile tugging at his lips.

She chuckled, shook her head. "Like you're exhausted. There's a room for visiting officers just past the bunk room. Settle in there and catch a few hours sleep before you leave."

He followed her advice, washing in the communal baths and taking the soft cotton pants and tunic Draper had given him so he had something to wear while the rest of his things were being cleaned, then collapsed onto the bed. It would be the only chance for a comfortable sleep he'd have for the foreseeable future.

He requested that the soldiers on duty wake him at change of guard at first light, and then he fell into a deep sleep.

"WAIT HERE."

Melodie heard the distrust and suspicion in the soldier's tone, and meekly accepted it with a nod.

She sat down on the long bench that was set against the wall in the front hall of the military barracks, hands folded in her lap.

She guessed they didn't have too many late-night visitors, and she had upset the usual order of things.

A woman came through the door, hair sticking up on one side, as if she had been dragged from bed. She stopped in front of Melodie. "I am Captain Ellen Draper, and I'm in charge of this barracks. My understanding was that Lieutenant Hallan and you had agreed that he was going to fetch you tomorrow morning."

Melodie looked up at her and nodded. "Yes." She didn't want to drag the sordid business between her and Vinest into the public, but from the glint in Captain Draper's eye, she decided honesty was probably the quickest way to get this over with. "My former employer didn't want me to leave and locked me in."

Draper's eyes narrowed. "Locked you in?"

"In my room. I lived with him over the workshop where I worked. I decided it would be better to escape tonight than delay the lieutenant tomorrow morning with an ugly confrontation." She lifted her shoulders. "I really just came to say I will try to get a room at the inn on the corner, and the lieutenant can fetch me there, rather than across the bridge tomorrow."

"Does your former employer know you are coming here?" Draper asked.

Melodie tilted her head, thinking about it. "He knows Theo is a soldier for Kassia and Cervantes; he has associated Theo with my leaving; so he may come here to ask questions." She thought back to what happened at the river crossing. "The soldiers at the booth in the middle of the bridge delayed him a little for me. I don't know if he decided to keep after me or not."

Draper glanced over at the soldier who had originally told

Melodie to wait. He had come back into the room and was standing to attention behind his captain. He nodded and moved to the door, slipping out into the night.

Gone to see what was happening at the bridge, Melodie guessed.

She was suddenly hit by a wave of fatigue. She forced herself to stand. "Please pass on my new address, Captain. I'll see Theo in the morning."

"You're from Kassia and Cervantes, aren't you?" Draper suddenly asked. "Even though you've come over from Grimwalt. I can hear it in your voice."

Melodie hesitated in the doorway. "I think so. But we moved around a lot when I was a child. My father never told me where we were originally from."

Theo suddenly pushed through the door from the back.

He was wearing soft black cotton pants and shirt, and it outlined the height and the breadth of him in fine detail. "Melodie."

She grimaced, suddenly feeling embarrassed and disheveled. "I didn't mean for you to be woken. I just wanted to say I left my house, and you can find me at the inn down the road tomorrow instead. Please go back to sleep."

"What happened?" he asked.

She shook her head. "It really doesn't matter. I'm packed and I'm ready. I'll see you tomorrow."

He moved, silent and quicker than someone that big surely should, and stopped her with a hand to her shoulder. "I knew something was wrong earlier, and I let you go into that house anyway. I'm sorry."

She stepped back, fighting the sudden prickle of tears. She would not weep. She would not look weak under the weight of so many suspicious eyes. "This was my fight, not yours. And it is finished. Go back to sleep." She drew in a breath, lifted a hand, and touched his arm. "Please."

As she turned to the door, Vinest burst in, hand clamping hard on her forearm. "There you are. We need to talk."

The look in his eyes was off, like he had lost some part of his sanity along the route from home to here.

She fixed her gaze on his fingers, knuckles white with the force he was using on her, and a sound came out of her throat in response to the pain that she couldn't control.

His head suddenly snapped back, and the bruising grip released.

She collapsed back onto the bench, arm cradled close to her stomach.

Theo had hit Vinest.

He was still hitting him.

"Enough." Draper came to stand beside Theo, and with a sound of regret he dropped his fists.

Vinest was hunched over by the door, arms lifted in front of his face.

"Let me see your arm," Draper ordered her.

The heat of embarrassment from earlier was nothing to what she felt now. She wanted to refuse, but the look on Draper's face told her she wouldn't take no for an answer. She extended her arm carefully, and Theo knelt beside her and carefully pushed up her jacket and her shirt sleeve.

The bruises already looked ugly, four lines on top, one below.

"I didn't mean to do that," Vinest said, gaze fixed on what he'd done. "I just want you back."

"You locked her up tonight, held her against her will?" Draper asked. "And now you have assaulted her in front of witnesses in the Kassia and Cervantes barracks."

Vinest was shaking his head. "I didn't plan to keep her locked up. I just wanted her to cool down, to rethink her plans."

"The law is clear," Draper said. "Locking someone up against their will is a crime that is always prosecuted in Kassia and Cervantes. It has to do with the fate of the Cervantes themselves at the hands of the old Kassian queen, and the life experience of the new queen, locked up for years by her cousin. There is no leniency, no mitigation you can give that will lessen the consequences. You're lucky the crime occurred in Grimwalt, or we would be delivering you to Public Security right now. Assault is also a crime here, though." Draper glanced at Melodie. "Do you want to press charges?"

Melodie looked down at her feet, still reeling that Vinest would do this to her, and then slowly lifted her head. "Yes. But I don't think I have time right now. Possibly when I return to Illoa, after my trip."

"What trip?" Vinest was looking at her with wild eyes. "Where are you going? I need you, Melodie. I made some miscalculations in the way I handled you, and I'm prepared to put them right."

"By locking her up and hurting her?" Theo's voice was soft and low, and Melodie shivered at the menace in it.

"No, no. I shouldn't have done that. I've made more bad decisions in the last ten hours than I have ever done before. Ask her! Ask her if I ever mistreated her before today."

Everyone turned to her, and she was suddenly sick of it. "He exploited me, he's been treating me like an indentured servant since I came to live with him, but this is the first time he's hurt me or tried to lock me up."

"Because this was the first time you wanted to walk away," Draper said.

"Yes," she answered.

"We have a place for you to sleep here tonight," Draper said. "Corporal Bindle will take you." She motioned with her hand, and Melodie saw four other soldiers had appeared in the room.

She shuffled forward, wishing she had simply left a note under the door earlier, and saved herself this mortification, and then, as she glanced at Vinest, at his pathetic face, she straightened.

She wasn't the one who should feel mortified, and if Vinest didn't, that was just more reason to keep far away from him.

"Thank you, Corporal," she said, as the soldier led her through into the back.

"All kinds of excitement today," the corporal said, with a quick grin. "And it's Jacinta." She was slender and muscular, dark hair braided down her back and dressed in sleeping clothes like the ones Theo had been wearing.

It looked like Melodie had gotten everyone out of bed.

Jacinta Bindle took her to a small room with two narrow beds set against each wall. "Sleep tight," she said. "I'll be part of the team traveling tomorrow, and I gather you're going with us." She paused. "I don't suppose you know what the big mystery is, do you?"

Melodie looked at her in surprise, and realized Theo hadn't told them. Or hadn't told the junior soldiers. Draper would most likely know.

"Ah. You do know but you can't say. Interesting." She left Melodie with a flick of her braid, and Melodie set down her bags and looked thoughtfully at the door.

She didn't know why she had thought she and Theo would be going alone, but now she wondered how she had come to that conclusion. Of course he would assemble a team.

They were going after Cervantes children who'd been abducted, who were being kept against their will.

As Draper had just explained, to these people, there was no greater crime.

CHAPTER 10

THEY SET OFF AFTER DAWN, allowing both her and Theo at least six hours of sleep.

There were four soldiers with them, all who shot quick, curious glances at her. She had been introduced to them when they had saddled up at the stables behind the barracks, but all that had been exchanged were their names.

She knew they were trying to work out why she was included in their party.

She was riding one of the loveliest mounts she'd had the pleasure to saddle up in many years. Her father had restricted their lives more and more toward the end, making them poorer and poorer, and she hadn't had access to a mount of this calibre in so long, she struggled to remember the last time she'd even ridden.

She stroked the horse's neck with affection and while she was probably going to be stiff by tonight, she was pleased she got back in the saddle as if she had never been out of it.

They were all equipped with tents and bed rolls, food and water. It was efficient and professional, and she could see why no one had dared lift a hand against Kassia and Cervantes since the Jatan had foolishly tried, just after the Rising Wave had taken the Kassian throne and installed their own queen in the castle.

She would have been around five years old then, and she didn't think anyone had tried again since.

They crossed the bridge and took the main route out to Taunen, Grimwalt's capital, and as soon as their group reached the first offset—a place for carts to stop for the night—Theo slowed his mount to a halt.

"You weren't told why you were assigned to come with me. The reason is because this is so sensitive, I couldn't risk even a whisper of it getting out."

Melodie noticed a few of the soldiers looked slightly insulted by the implication, but they all kept their attention on the lieutenant.

"Myself and General Bardet were on roster for the novice fortnight." He paused, and Melodie could see what he was about to say truly pained him. "It was the last two nights, where they make camp on their own and build a small bridge over a stream, or a lookout post."

The soldiers were nodding along, as if this was a good memory for them.

"Someone kidnapped them." Theo's words jerked them out of their reverie.

"Took them?" Jacinta Bindle almost whispered it.

"Took them by force," Theo said. "They tried to fight back, but they were overcome."

The whole group was utterly still.

"General Bardet is riding hard down to Ta-lin to call for help. I followed the trail I picked up at their camp, and I ran the abductor to ground." A breeze had sprung up, tugging at clothing, lifting hair, but no one moved.

"The children were all accounted for, lying tied up around a fire. I couldn't see their abductor or abductors, so I moved around the camp, looking for signs of danger." He made a movement, an almost involuntary jerk of remembered helplessness. "Someone snuck up behind me, and we fought. I got in a strike, but I was also struck down. Not with a weapon, with a spell. We are dealing with a magic user. A spell caster."

One of the other soldiers, someone Melodie had been introduced to as Gallain, made a sound at the back of his throat.

Theo acknowledged it with a nod. "He spelled me to become a goat."

After a moment of surprise, Caro, another of their group, leaned forward on her horse. "Did you say a goat?"

Theo lifted his shoulders. "I didn't know what spell was caging me at first. It took a while to come back to myself, but somehow I ended up in the hands of another trader. He then tied me to the Malin bridge on the Grimwalt side."

"How did you get free?" The soldier who asked was Ivan. He was the biggest of them all, bigger than Theo, even, and he had said almost nothing until now.

"Melodie set me free." Theo nodded toward her, and suddenly four pairs of eyes swung in her direction. "Melodie can see spell work, and that is why she is with us. She will help us defeat this particular enemy."

"How long were you bespelled?" Caro held herself straight in her saddle, as if ready to gallop off at a moment's notice.

"At least two days," Theo said. "We are on the back foot in all respects."

"And how do you come into it, Melodie?" Jacinta asked. "Where are you from?" Her tone was suspicious, her eyes challenging.

"I work at the jewelers on Eisen Street." Melodie held her gaze. "I was shopping at the stalls in the Grimwalt square."

"And you just happened to notice a goat that was really a man?" Ivan sounded skeptical.

She hesitated. She found it so hard to speak about this. But they needed to trust her. They were headed into danger, and they needed to know she was telling the truth, needed to believe her when she warned them about something.

"As Theo says, I can see spell work. The spell that held Theo was very bright. I could see it across the square. And I could see it was embedded in a piece of copper twine around his neck. I got him to a private place and cut him free."

They stared at her, this time more thoughtful than shocked.

"Why are you a jeweler?" Caro asked. "Why aren't you working for a court somewhere?"

"What do you think a spell caster like the one we're tracking would think of someone like me?" Melodie asked. "How safe would I be walking around if it was well-known?" She looked over at Theo. "He caught a Cervantes warrior who was looking out for danger. How easily would he have caught me?"

There was a moment of silence.

"Point taken." Gallain cleared his throat.

"Does the jeweler who runs the workshop on Eisen Street know? Is that why he was so desperate to keep you there?" Jacinta asked.

She had hoped they wouldn't bring that up, but now that they had, she faced it. "No. He doesn't know. I'm just a very good jewelry designer."

Caro gave a low chuckle at that, and Melodie shot her a smile.

"Melodie has answered enough questions." Theo chopped his hand downward, as if cutting off any more discussion. "We need to catch up to the trader who tied me to the bridge. He can't be far. He told Melodie he was going to spend the night just outside the city, and then he was headed for Taunen. I don't think he planned to take the main road."

They all looked toward Taunen, and Melodie saw Theo rubbing the back of his neck in agitation.

"You couldn't have gone after him last night," she said. "You needed to recover."

He glanced at her as if to deny it, then gave a tight nod.

"You think he spent the night right here?" Caro asked, looking at the thin strip of grass they were gathered on.

"I do." Theo slid off his horse and crouched by the blackened stones surrounding a small fire pit. "The stones are still warm, and the horse droppings are fresh."

"The first turn-off to a minor road is at least an hour's ride from here," Victor said. "If he's in a slow cart, we can catch him."

Theo swung back into the saddle. "Then let's catch him."

CHAPTER 11

THEY CAUGHT up with the trader after forty minutes of hard riding.

He must have been on the road since before sunrise to have managed to get so far, but their horses were well-kept and fast, and his donkey was old, and pulling a heavy caravan.

Theo could see he looked confused, until he saw Melodie, and then he went white.

He jumped down from the driver's bench and ran off into the field beside the road.

The group converged, horses blowing from the hard ride, some dancing around in agitation.

"We going after him?" Ivan asked.

"I will." Melodie slid off her mount and tossed the reins to Jacinta. "I'm the one he knows."

"I'll come." Theo had no intention of letting her go alone.

"Me, too." Gallain dismounted.

"No, keep watch on the road, and maybe search the caravan while we're gone. He won't be any trouble," Theo said.

Gallain looked like he wanted to argue, but he wasn't in charge and he gave a reluctant nod.

Melodie crossed to the side and hopped over a narrow ditch, then started off through the long grass.

Theo followed close behind.

The old man stood watching them from a small copse to the right of the field, waiting but tense, as if ready to run again. That would not do.

Theo caught up to Melodie and reached back to grip the pommel of the sword Draper had given him from the armory.

The trader saw him do it, and Theo could tell the moment he gave up all thoughts of running.

He looked down, then slumped against the tree and let his knees fold and take him to the ground.

Melodie glanced back at Theo in surprise, as if trying to work out why their quarry had surrendered, saw his grip on his sword, and gave a tiny nod of comprehension.

"I don't know what it does," the old man called out as they approached. "I should have destroyed it."

For a moment, Theo couldn't understand what he was talking about, and then realized he must think this was about the paint set.

Melodie lifted a shoulder as she got close enough to talk quietly. "We aren't here about that."

The old man looked up, confused, and then glanced across the field to the rest of their group. "Is this about the goat?" He almost squeaked out the words.

"In a way," Theo said, coming to stand beside Melodie. "I want to know the story of how you came by the goat, and why you left it tied to the bridge."

The old man looked between him and Melodie, and started shaking his head. "I don't know—"

"You do," Melodie interrupted him gently. "Telling the truth, no matter what it is, will bring no trouble on you. Only the opposite is true."

"You're telling me stealing is not a crime in Grimwalt?" he asked, voice laced with sarcasm.

"But we aren't Grimwaldian," Theo told him. "We have no authority here to impose the laws. We are after the man who had the paints and the goat. We want to find him very much."

"Who are you, if you aren't Grimwaldian?" His voice quavered.

"Kassia and Cervantes," Theo answered. "We know you came across him on the other side of Grimwalt's border. You worry about being arrested as a thief. The man we're talking about stole something much more valuable than magic paints and a goat."

"You will let me go on my way?"

"If you answer truthfully." Melodie tilted her head back, eyes narrowed. "You saw something when you stole the paints."

He looked at her with such shock, Theo had to believe she was completely right. The old man did know something.

"Quick, now. Tell us, and we'll leave you to go on your way." Melodie waved a hand impatiently. "It's important."

"Who are you?" He was still suspicious.

"What do we look like?" Theo asked.

The trader pointed at the others, waiting on the road, then at him. "You look military. She . . ." He glanced at Melodie. "She looks like a sweet young woman who shouldn't be mixed up with the likes of you."

Melodie crouched down. "You stole from him, and he will not forget it. Ever. That's why you left the Grimwalt market square after only one day. That's why you're already on the road, so early. You know he will come for you. Tell us what you know, and with luck, we will deal with him for you."

The old man stared at her for a long moment, then let out a shuddering breath. "If he finds out I told . . ."

"He won't find out." Melodie was firm.

"You know what the paint box does?" The trader sounded both skeptical and curious.

"I do. Now tell us."

The man hesitated, then looked at Theo, and winced. Cleared his throat hurriedly. "I came across a camp fire on my way to Illoa. I had had a wheel break earlier in the day and it took a long time to fix, so I pushed my journey later into the night than usual to get to the town. I saw the fire and realized I was still too far to make it that night, and went to join fellow travelers." He paused. "There was a goat standing over some figures sleeping around the fire, and an old man who had been attacked with a knife or a sword lying on the ground."

He pushed himself to his feet, looked at Theo again, and then sank back down to his haunches. "I didn't want trouble, and so I was just going to leave, but I thought the goat might be good for milk, and there was a small bag at the back of the cart, so I took both and left."

He looked up cautiously.

"And?" Melodie tapped fingers on the top of her hand, reminding him to hurry.

"And once I was on my way and had a chance to look through the bag, I found the paints, and a letter from someone in Bartolo to someone called Marchant in Warven." He waved his hand to the left. "I've heard of Warven before, it's on the way to Taunen, but off the main road. About two days by cart from Illoa."

"What was the letter about?" Theo asked.

"It said there was an item Marchant would find extremely interesting, but the man in Bartolo—I can't remember the name— would not send it via courier. He said it was worth too much, and if Marchant wanted it, he would have to come and get it himself or send a proxy." The merchant shrugged. "I guessed the paint box was that item. And that Marchant had bought it, and was on his way back home."

That sounded like a logical explanation. Marchant would have passed close to the children's camp on the road from Bartolo to Illoa. This was most likely a chance event, not a premeditated kidnapping of the princess.

"Where, exactly, in Warven was the letter addressed to?" Melodie asked.

The old man shook his head. "It was addressed care of the inn in Warven."

Theo glanced over at the road, and noticed the others getting restless. "If you've lied to us," he said, "I will find you. Do I make myself clear?"

The trader gripped his hands together. "Aye."

"Good." Theo stepped away, but Melodie stayed where she was.

"Why did you tie the goat to the bridge?" she asked.

"Because it turned out to be a billy goat, and I wasn't going to get any milk out of it. I didn't want to just abandon it, though. Thought people might feed it by the bridge, or it could eat the apples there. And maybe someone would take it home."

"I'm glad you did that, at least," Melodie said.

Theo looked back, caught her gaze, and with a shrug, she moved to join him.

"Wait." The old man's voice trembled a little. "Be careful of that box."

"It's a bit late now, old man," she told him, glancing over her shoulder, and then she strode toward the road.

Theo fell in step with her.

"You really know what the paint box does?" he asked, just before they reached the others.

"How do you think I escaped my old boss?" she asked.

He reached out and gripped her arm. "You used it?"

She patted his forearm with her other hand, her eyes alight with amused laughter at his concern. "It's not made by *him*," she said. "Sounds like he bought it from someone in Bartolo."

"Will it hurt him not to have it?" Theo asked.

She considered the question. "It is useful, so the answer to that is probably yes."

All right then. He released his hold on her.

"I'll show you, if you like?" she said.

"When?"

"Tonight, when we make camp." She grabbed the reins Jacinta tossed her and swung back in the saddle.

"We're going to Warven, wherever that is," Theo told the team, who were watching his and Melodie's byplay with interest.

"I know of it," said Gallain.

"Then lead the way."

CHAPTER 12

THEY RODE HARD, so when they finally stopped for the night, Melodie wasn't surprised that they mostly brushed down and fed their horses in silence.

"You ride well enough," Jacinta said to her as Melodie put her saddle down with the rest of the group's. "Didn't think you would."

"I spent a lot of time riding when I was younger," she said. "But I'm feeling how long it's been already."

She tried to not let the stiffness show too much, but Jacinta flashed her a sympathetic grin as they found seats around the fire that Ivan had started.

The provisions Draper had given them required no cooking—dried fruit and meat, cheese and fresh bread.

They all pulled what they wanted from their bags and silence descended as they ate and waited for the water in the pot Ivan had hung over the fire to boil.

Melodie found a cup in her bag, the same as everyone else, and held it out as Ivan poured the tea.

"What did you tell the lieutenant you'd show him tonight?" Caro asked.

Melodie hadn't realized they'd heard the details of her and Theo's conversation, but she'd assumed she would show him in front of the others, anyway.

There were uses for this she might not think of, and it was a weapon in their combined arsenal. It would be good to have everyone aware of it.

"The trader stole something from the spell caster—whose name is most likely Marchant."

"How come he didn't see the children?" Caro asked.

Melodie looked over to Theo, who was watching her silently, sipping from his mug. "He did," she said. "He says he thought they were sleeping."

Caro looked skeptical, but she gave a nod of acceptance.

"What did he steal?"

"This." Melodie took it out of her bag. "A box of watercolor paints."

Everyone leaned closer.

"And what's special about them?" Gallain asked.

"If you draw something, it becomes real," she said. "When my former boss locked me in my room on the top floor of the house, I drew rope and climbed out of the window."

There was complete silence now.

"Show us." Theo rose up and came to sit right next to her.

She took out a piece of paper, flipped it over to the blank side, and got out her brush and her bowl. She poured some water into it.

"What do you think would be useful to draw?" she asked.

"A knife." Ivan was sitting on her other side, and he leaned closer, too.

"That's a good one." She nodded.

She drew a knife the full length of the page, angling the paper to see better in the dancing firelight. The others crowded around behind her, looking over her shoulder.

When she was done, she put it on the ground near the fire. "It needs to dry."

"And then?" Theo asked. He hadn't lifted his gaze from her work since she'd started painting.

"Then it vanishes off the page and becomes real." As she said it, the fire dried the last of the water, and the paper was suddenly weighed down by the leather-handled knife she had drawn.

"Fuck me." Ivan picked it up, tested the blade, and sucked in a quick, surprised breath at the sharpness.

Everyone took their seat, and Ivan passed it around, so everyone could feel and see it.

While they did it, Melodie counted under her breath.

Theo was the last to get it, and he turned it from every angle.

"Does it disappear?" he asked.

She nodded, suddenly counting out loud, and as she hit six hundred, it vanished in his hands.

Theo glanced at her. "How did you know?"

"The rope vanished while I was using it to climb down. Fortunately, I didn't have far to fall."

Theo studied her. "Was that the first thing you drew?"

She gave a wry smile. "I drew a key to unlock my door," she said. "It didn't fit. I think it would have to have been an exact replica of the actual key, and I didn't know what it looked like."

"So if we come to a locked door, you can't just draw a key that will magically work," Jacinta said.

"No. That's why I've done this demonstration. To show you what it can do, but to also let you know what it can't do. It's useful, but it has its limitations."

"Still, it's a lot better than nothing," Caro mused. "I can see uses for it."

"And you're sure it isn't somehow linked to the spell caster?" Theo looked at the box as he spoke. "It can't be turned on us, somehow?"

"I don't know," she answered. "I don't think so. I think it's neutral, and something he acquired."

The others had obviously not even thought of that possibility, and they were looking at the paints a little more warily.

"Can any of you draw?" she asked, to break the moment. "Would you like to give it a go?"

Gallain stood. "I'm not bad," he admitted. "But I usually draw landscapes."

"We don't want to waste paint." Theo took the box from her and studied it. "Some colors are half-used up."

"We need to think of things that are useful, but that we only need for a short time," Melodie said.

"My horse picked up a stone during the ride," Caro said. "I tried to get it out, but it's lodged in too tightly."

"I know what you need." Melodie took the paints and the paper back, and quickly painted one of the tools her father used all the time. Theo leaned a little closer to look.

"I've seen that before. You know your farrier's tools."

"My father was a blacksmith." She held the paper out, close to the fire, and between one moment and the next, it appeared on top of the page.

"I was watching that, and it was suddenly there, faster than a blink." Ivan took it off the paper, weighed it in his hand.

"Use it quickly, or it'll disappear," Theo warned them, and Ivan and Caro moved to the horses at a fast clip.

"That's why you're a silver and goldsmith?" Gallain asked. "Because your father was a blacksmith?"

Melodie nodded. "It was a trade I knew, and my father organized an apprenticeship with Lorn Vinest. He died a few weeks after I started there, and Vinest took me in to live with him."

"He never tried to keep you locked in before?" Theo was leaning forward, elbows on his knees, his head turned toward her.

The firelight played on his face and made his hair gleam, and for a moment she couldn't think.

She managed to shake her head, and then forced herself to look into the fire. "I did what he wanted until yesterday, so he had no reason to. But I've been unhappy there for a while."

"And you're sure he doesn't know?" Theo asked. "That you can see spell work?"

She shook her head again. "I never told him. My father died trying to make sure no one ever knew." She raised her head and caught Gallain and Jacinta's eyes. "I have to trust you will keep my secret."

"We don't take your trust lightly." Gallain was the one who spoke. "You are helping us get our children back."

Jacinta murmured her assent, and then Ivan and Caro returned.

"It worked, and just in time." Caro rubbed her fingers together. "Felt really strange as it faded away."

"The paints are a tool we can use, if we think strategically," Melodie said. "And, maybe even more importantly, it is something that is no longer in the spell caster's hands."

Theo nodded. "That is definitely something I do like about it." He tapped his knees, the movement fast and restless.

Melodie wondered if he wished they didn't have to let the horses rest.

"We need to sleep. And we need to be ready for anything." Theo stood. "I'll take first watch. Melodie doesn't have military training, so she doesn't have guard duty. Caro, you're second watch. Ivan is third. Gallain, you're fourth. Jacinta gets a full night's sleep, and that will rotate.

There were a few groans, but Melodie thought they were for show.

Within twenty minutes, everyone had set up their beds, and Theo left to do a walk around.

She was already half asleep when she heard a stick crack beneath a boot, and lifted her head to find herself looking straight at Theo. He was standing at the outer edges of light thrown by the fire, watching her.

She gave him a solemn nod, and he returned it, then turned away, disappearing into the darkness.

She snuggled down and breathed out, trying to quiet her mind. She was exhausted from the ride, but the combination of the strangeness of being back on the road after years of barely moving from the workshop, the strange feeling of fascination she felt for

Theo, and the sickening thought of children in the hands of someone who meant them harm, rattled about in her head.

She heard a low feminine murmur, a deeper male response, then a log cracked and popped on the fire, and she was drawn back in time to the travels with her father, the groups they'd joined for safety, and the nights just like this, around the fire. And she slept.

CHAPTER 13

Viviane looked up at the dark stone of the ceiling, at the wispy spider webs clinging to the corners, and forced herself to confront her new reality.

She had been captured. Bested.

Her mother and father had both told her and her little brother stories of how they had been taken—it was how her parents had met, in a dungeon in northern Kassia.

But she had never considered that it could happen to her.

She had been protected far more than she realized, she saw now. And it hurt her sense of strength and confidence that not just herself, but all four of them, had been so easily grabbed.

Theo and Uncle Rafe would be looking for them. She had a strange dream, one that she almost dared not examine too closely, where Theo had caught up to them, had circled around the fire where they lay, and then had been bested, too.

It was too terrible to think about, and the fact that he wasn't with them now gave her just enough hope that it was a nightmare. Enough to calm the panic that kept rising up in her.

She kept reminding herself she was not without weapons.

This madman thought they were all magical. He kept muttering it under his breath. He didn't know the half of it.

He had left them in their night clothes. He'd taken their other clothes, and their boots, too, fingering the cloak her mother had given her with thoughtful interest. She had lain helpless while he'd laughed out loud as he gathered it up. She knew her mother had woven all kinds of protections into it, but she hadn't been wearing it when she had been taken—it had been in the middle of the night and she'd been asleep inside her tent.

They had all gotten filthy and wet while they built the bridge across the stream, and so most of their clothes had been hanging around the fire to dry.

It had been so much fun, that last day, they'd melded as a true team, and Vivi had the sense they would be friends for life.

When they'd sat around the fire before bed and played the secrets game, she had been so tempted to tell them the biggest secret of all.

She was very glad now she had not.

Their abductor must have been watching them, listening to them. He had struck moments after they'd climbed into their tents, and from a few of the comments he'd made, she was sure he'd been watching them the night before, too.

Because she kept quiet and never said anything to her friends, he didn't know what she could do.

Although he knew she could do something. He thought they all could.

Her mother had said more than once that while her father was theoretically not magical, the way he moved—the way all the Cervantes moved—made her think their magic was built into their very bodies.

And that was before her mother had sewn magic into her father's skin.

This terrible person, this abductor-spell worker, could sense that magic in her friends. Vivi was half Cervantes, half Grimwaldian, and she had inherited her mother's magic. The others were all

Cervantes, born and bred, and she had thought she was the only magical member of the group. It was a lesson in assumptions for her. A lesson in respecting the inherent magic her mother thought resided in her father's people.

Their abductor told them he collected magical things. And for all he had managed to take them all with barely any trouble, he looked old and sick. His eyes blinked often, as if he had trouble seeing, and he moved as if his joints ached.

He kept going on about how amazed he'd been to find they all had some power. They were his biggest haul.

He had rubbed hands together as he said it, and smiled that horrible smile.

He was gone now.

He'd left them in a stone cell, herself and Genevieve chained to the wall closest to the barred door, with Jonquil and Ricardo chained to the wall at the back, with a long wooden bench along each wall for them to lie or sit on. There were chains enough for two more people—a fifth and sixth were looped up high on the wall opposite. The whole fourth wall, that ran along the front of the room, was simply metal bars all the way across with a door made up of the same bars set into it for access.

It meant he could see exactly what they were up to as soon as he came in.

He seemed to also be able to see magic, and so she suppressed her first thought, which was at least to braid protection into her hair. It would only give her away that much faster.

He'd left—she didn't see him go, but she'd heard the creak and then slam of a door—so that the only sound was the labored breathing of her friends.

She hadn't been able to breathe very well herself, but she was improving. It had been the most frightening experience of her life, being unable to so much as twitch a finger—aware and awake but frozen in place, trying to force air in and out of her lungs.

She had been staring up at the ceiling for a while when Genevieve made a sound behind her. Viviane almost didn't realize the significance of being able to twist her head back to look at her, but when she realized she could finally move, she tried to sit up.

She rolled off the bench instead, but she didn't mind the pain of landing on the cold stone floor. She was getting the use of her body back.

And every breath came more easily.

"Gen, you all right?" she managed to wheeze.

Genevieve's answer was a desperate choking sound, as if she tried to speak and coughed instead.

"Shh," Vivi whispered. "Take your time. Whatever he did to us, it's loosening its hold."

Across the room, Jon sucked in a rattling breath. "Fuck me."

Jon liked to swear, and they teased him about it, but right now, Vivi couldn't think of a more on point description of their situation.

"Ric?" she managed to get out.

Jon coughed. "Looks like he's asleep."

"Ric stabbed him," Vivi suddenly remembered. "With a sharp stick. Maybe he did something more to him than the rest of us."

"Where are we?" Gen whispered.

Vivi felt a wave of relief at hearing her speak. "I don't know."

"Why does he keep saying we're magic?" Jon asked, voice more hushed now, in line with Gen's.

"I don't know," she said again. "But it's not good."

Ric suddenly drew in a whistling breath, and Viviane finally managed to struggle up to a seated position. She moved slowly, like the old men and women in the Fernwell market, got onto her hands and knees, and crawled toward him.

The chain on her ankle yanked her back just before she reached him.

She stretched out her hand, but she couldn't touch him.

Jon finally managed to move a little. He swung his legs down so he was sitting on the bench, then shuffled along it. He heaved himself up and used a hand against the wall to steady himself until he was standing over his friend.

He pushed weakly at his shoulder, finally managing to get him on his side, and Vivi sat back on her heels with relief when she heard Ric's breathing ease.

"This is an actual dungeon," Gen said, as if finally noticing where they were. "Or at least a prison cell."

"Yes." Viviane slowly crawled back to the bench and heaved herself up. This was an actual cell, and it looked well used.

They were not the first occupants.

Viviane wanted to make sure they were the last.

CHAPTER 14

Theo knew he had been a hard taskmaster, that he'd forced everyone almost beyond their limits.

Especially Melodie.

She wasn't a trained soldier, and from what she'd told him, she spent long hours sitting at her workshop bench.

She wasn't used to riding, let alone riding all day.

He had seen her fall asleep almost immediately the night before, and he had watched her more than once on his guard rounds. He'd set up his sleeping mat on the far side of the camp to her when it was his turn to sleep. His fascination with her was a little too distracting, so he forced himself to keep his distance.

They had ridden on the road to Warven until about midday, and then Gallain had taken them off it, through open fields leading to the distant hill he said stood above the town.

On horseback, without a cart, it would be a much faster route.

Caro had protested as they'd struggled over rocky ground for a bit, but the way got smoother, and Theo hadn't been able to stop himself from riding ahead. Whenever he'd looked back, he'd noticed Melodie lagging further and further behind the group, but now, looking down the slope as the others emerged from the tree-line of the forest that skirted the hill, he saw she was not even in view.

He had meant to stop a few times to wait for her, and he wasn't quite sure now why he hadn't.

He slid off his mount and gave it a rub down while he waited for the others to catch up.

They took the narrow path in single file, but even when they had almost reached him, Melodie was still out of sight.

He tried to remember why he'd stopped here, and then he heard the stream and recalled it was to water the horses. As soon as his horse was brushed down he led it over to drink its fill and then let it loose to pull at the thick green grasses that grew on the bank.

"Did you go the last bit up the hill to see Warven below?" Gallain asked as he slid off his horse.

Theo shook his head. "I heard the stream, then I looked back and couldn't see Melodie with you. No sense going further until she's caught up."

While they rubbed their horses down and then watered them, Theo got a small fire going and boiled some water, acting on the ingrained routine of many journeys.

One by one the others drifted over and found a place to sit or lie, and eat something from their provisions.

They moved without urgency, and he had a moment of wondering at that.

When he looked at what food he had left, he turned to Gallain. "Warven is over the hill and below, and we can restock down there?"

"Yes." Gallain chewed some bread and cheese and Caro got up and made tea.

"Still no sign of Melodie?" Ivan asked.

Theo shook his head. He was keeping an eye on the slope, and she still wasn't visible.

"She's not fit enough for the pace you set," Jacinta said. "Not her fault, but she didn't say anything, so she fell behind."

"She's used to trying to please," Caro agreed. "I think she's been trained to not cause trouble or be noticed and she tries to do what's asked of her, even if it's unreasonable. She should have asked us to slow down for her, but it isn't in her upbringing to do that."

"That explanation took an unexpected turn." Ivan frowned, as if disturbed by the bluntness of the comments, then stretched out his legs, wriggled until he was lying flat on the ground. "It sounds like we're trying to excuse ourselves, because we should have waited for her. We're professional soldiers, she's a civilian."

"We should have waited," Jacinta agreed. "I forgot to look back, because it was all I could do to keep up myself."

"This is my fault, no one else's." Theo pushed himself to his feet. "I knew she didn't have the fitness level, but I didn't keep an eye on her. I'll go back to find her."

"We might end up staying the night here, then," Gallain finally spoke up. "It's already late in the day."

"We can't go on without her. We could walk straight into a magical trap. And we know we're dealing with someone who can do that." Theo didn't like the thought of her being on her own, being left behind, either. This was really on him. He felt strangely removed from the decision to not watch her more closely.

He'd been so focused on reaching Warven, he hadn't taken care of one of his most important assets.

Even that thought made him wince. She *was* an asset, but she was also a person who had intrinsic value.

And he had not taken the care with her that he should have.

"Your horse needs to rest," Caro said.

"I know. I'll walk." They had two hours before the sun set, and that should be enough time to reach her and get back.

Unless she was far further behind than he thought.

He jogged down the hill, pleased to be off his horse for a bit, stretching his legs.

He loved to run, and he and the Commander often ran together, especially when they were stationed at Fernwell, and horses were less necessary than when they were at Ta-lin.

Of the two centers of power, one in Kassia, one in Cervantes, he loved Ta-lin more, the open plains and wooded valleys called to him, but Fernwell held its charms, too. The shouts from the merchant ships in the harbor, the smell of the sea and the strange and delicious scents from the marketplace made it an interesting place to be.

He had trained with his uncle, Rafe, since he was twelve. It was the earliest his mother, Rafe's sister, would allow him to. The Chosen camps had only been destroyed a few years earlier, and his parents had spent his childhood in fear of him being taken—until the Commander and his uncle, and their friends, had broken free and turned the tables.

He was self-aware enough to realize his focus on being strong and deadly, the best Cervantes warrior he could be, was rooted in that childhood fear, that worry of being taken.

And that focus had helped him through the ranks.

He was the youngest lieutenant in the military, and there were a few grumbles that his uncle's deep friendship with the Commander had given him a leg up, but those grumbles quietened when he challenged the mutterers to a training bout.

Perhaps some of the hard training he put himself through was in part due to the worry that they were right. Luc Franck was someone he had dinner with regularly. There was a special friendship between himself and Queen Ava, and in private he dropped her title altogether when talking to her, at her own insistence.

While he knew Ricardo, Jonquil, and Genevieve, the three students who'd been taken, he was like an older cousin to Viviane, and he had to admit the burning drive to go faster, to ride harder, was down to his terror at what might be happening to her.

He had let that worry blind him to Melodie's limitations. She had done well the day before, but only someone who rode regularly could keep up with the advanced pace he'd set.

He had brought her along because he didn't think he could be successful without her, so he was truly a fool to lose her.

When he reached the tree line he slowed, checking to make

sure he was on the right path, and then wondered if Melodie had fallen so far behind she had taken a wrong turn.

If they'd kept to the road, that wouldn't have been a worry, but as soon as they went off on Gallain's shortcut, he should have made sure they kept together.

He cursed himself again for his negligence and began calling her name as he stepped into the dark cool beneath the canopy.

The sun was setting behind the hill, and it was already hard to see the way.

He listened for a response to his call, and was met with silence.

CHAPTER 15

Melodie had been left behind. And it was partly her own fault.

It had felt like she was in some kind of muddled nightmare as they'd approached the forest, and then the wind had changed, and she got a second wind, or at least, became more aware of her surroundings.

When she reached the tree line that had swallowed up the rest of the team earlier, she slowed the horse to a walk and let the cool green gloom of the forest soothe the headache she suddenly realized she'd had for hours as she took stock.

She slid out of the saddle and listened for the others, and when she heard nothing, she looked at the forest floor, and began following the hoof prints she found here and there.

The rest of the group had been going fast, and where the ground was damp, the horses' hooves were clearly visible.

She felt a little frisson of relief at the sight of them, and with the relief came a spike of anger. If she had held them up, they would have to accept some of the blame for leaving her so far behind.

It was actually wonderful to be out of the saddle, stretching her legs in a gentle walk. The breeze lifted her hair off her face and she breathed in the spicy scent of pine. When she remembered she needed to be watching for hoof prints, she forced herself to look down and concentrate, and found there were none.

She had lost the path.

She stopped, closing her eyes again to listen carefully.

The leaves above her head rustled, and she could hear a bird calling the same two notes over and over, to her left. Behind her, something small scurried over dead leaves.

With a shiver of branches, the wind changed direction again, and as she opened her eyes, darkness seemed to fall all at once. She'd seen the hill rising above the forest as she'd approached, so it made sense that the sun had slipped behind it, and thrown the trees into shadow.

It was later than she'd thought. Surely the others would have realized by now that she was not behind them.

As her eyes adjusted to the gloom, she noticed tiny sparkles of light drifting all around her, dancing on the breeze likes sparks from a fire.

She frowned at the sight of them, trying to work out what they were.

The sun was gone, so this wasn't light on dust.

She held out her hand and two sparkles landed on her palm.

Magic.

She ran a fingertip over the tiny lights, and was enveloped in confusion.

She gasped as the ring on her finger suddenly burned her, and she flicked the sparks away. She leaned against her horse until she felt less disoriented. The ring still itched, but it no longer hurt her.

A trap.

This was a trap, set to confuse.

She wondered where it originated, and then watched as a sparkle rode the air currents toward her, and landed on her sleeve. She hadn't seen the sparkles before it got dark—the light through the trees had made it too difficult—but given the feeling of disorientation she'd felt when they'd touched her skin, she wondered what their effect was if they were breathed in.

Not good, was her guess.

She untied her pack and found the handkerchief with protection embroidered into it. It might not be made for her, but it would work to keep the sparkles out if she tied it over her mouth and nose. She pulled on some gloves.

Feeling less nervous, she walked forward, watching the sparkles and trying to discern a direction. They seemed to be floating from east to west, using the wind, and she took the next path eastward, until she heard the faint tinkle of a stream.

Her horse snorted, and she stroked its neck. "I know. I'm thirsty, too."

She found the stream and filled her water bottle, letting her horse drink.

The sparkles were more obvious here, where the trees drew denser around the water source, and the shadows were darker.

There were also more of them in the air—they looked like clouds of midges—and she left the horse to graze and jumped the narrow stream, heading toward their source.

She wondered how affected the others had been by the magic, and whether the man they were after had already captured them.

She'd gotten lost. Maybe they had, too.

She pushed her way through two trees whose trunks crossed above her head, and found a small, open space, not even big enough to call a clearing, with an open box on the ground.

There were leaves and debris around it, piled up on all sides as if they weren't able to fall into the box itself, and the tiny lights spiraled up from within like sparks from a fire, swirling in the breeze and dancing away in the darkness.

She circled the box, trying to find a way to look inside without standing directly over it. She was sure if sparkles landed in her eyes, she would forget why she was even here.

She crouched, waddling awkwardly closer and feeling the strain of muscles too long in the saddle.

The lid was almost hidden by leaves and twigs, and she reached out gingerly, got her fingers under the top of it, and flicked it with a hard, upward jerk.

It lifted, stopped halfway to closing, and then flipped back.

She chewed the inside of her cheek while she considered her next move.

The sparkles were still dancing away, flying westward, and she lay down on the east side and wriggled even closer. When she was almost close enough for her nose to touch the side, she began to blow gently, and the sparkles, instead of first rising up before being carried away, caught the breeze immediately.

She peered over the edge to look inside, and saw a glowing crystal. She backed away, keeping low to the ground, and found a rock.

While she was working her way back to the box, she heard someone blundering through the trees, and then heard them call her name.

Theo.

He was walking directly into the stream of sparkles, and the fact that she could hear him at all told her how disoriented he was—she had noticed last night when he was on guard duty just how quietly he could move.

She ignored his approach—the quicker she dealt with this, the better it would be for them both—and finally managed to reach the box.

She drew up slightly to give herself some height, blowing steadily again, but as if it felt her intent, the sparkles whisked upward and blew straight into her face. She could feel them as tiny, hot pricks of magic, and she fell back.

Theo emerged from between the trees, leaning against one of the trunks, and blinking at her in confusion.

"How are you at throwing accurately?" she asked him, and the words were hard to get out of her mouth.

"Pretty good," he said, after a moment's thought.

"Come round to my side then," she said.

He blundered through the sparkles as if he couldn't see them, and his foot caught the pile of leaves and debris on one side of the box and scattered them in an explosion of dust.

He must have breathed some in, because he started to cough, wheezing by the time he reached her.

"Been looking for you," he said. He crouched beside her and ran a hand over her hair in a strange, intimate caress. "Been worried."

She tried to remember something about him, about why she should be surprised by his touch, then let her head flop back to rest in his palm. "We have to throw a rock into that box."

"All right." He took the rock she handed him and stared at the box for a long moment. Then he threw, and it whipped through the air, reached the box and then seemed to bounce off an invisible barrier. It landed to the side and then rolled away.

She had forgotten that the leaves couldn't land in there. Obviously a rock couldn't, either.

She would have to crawl back and smash it herself.

Since Theo had thrown the rock, even more sparkles had risen up, and they blew toward them.

She felt lightheaded, and when her vision cleared a little she realized they were lying in each other's arms, in the crook of a tree root.

The sparkles were less now, whisked away by a stiffening breeze, and she squinted a little at the box, content to lie in Theo's embrace.

"I like it here," he said.

She nuzzled the skin of his neck through the handkerchief that was still covering her mouth and nose, and sighed. She wanted to move the handkerchief away, feel his skin against her lips, but remembered she should keep her mouth covered. She tried to remember why. "I like it here, too, but I have to close the box. Or break what's inside it."

"I can help you." He ran a hand down her arm, pulling her a little closer.

She closed her eyes, and slowly found herself less lethargic.

"Do you have a handkerchief?" she asked.

He patted his pockets absently, and then brought one out with a flourish.

It was bigger than her own, and she struggled up, pulling it over her head and then knotting two corners just below her eyes.

He was more confused than she was, but that's because she still wore the mouth covering, and she could see the sparkles. She was aware of what was happening to her. And confused as he was, he was willing to help her, and listen to her.

As long as she understood what to do, they could get out of this.

"Pull me back if I fall," she told him, and then she got on her hands and knees and crawled to where the rock had landed.

She moved back to him, and handed it over.

"Can you hit the side of the box?" If it couldn't go in, it could hopefully knock the box over. "The side where you kicked the leaves away?"

Theo pushed up on an elbow, lifted the rock, and spun it like he was skipping stones on a lake.

It hit the box with a crack, and it flipped over.

The sparkles winked out, trapped beneath the overturned box.

She smiled and snuggled down in his arms. The air was clear now, and she pulled the handkerchief off her head and the one around her mouth down around her neck. Kissed his cheek.

"What was that for?" he murmured.

"For your great aim."

Neither of them spoke for long minutes, and she gave a sigh and sat up. "That was so strange."

He was watching her with eyes that were clear now, rather than dreamy. "Magic?" he asked.

"A confusion trap. It's still going, inside that box, so we'll have to find a way to stop it." She looped her arms around her knees, in no hurry to stand, and looked at the box a little more.

"You got caught in it, too?" he asked.

"It was hard to see it until the sun went behind the hill, because the magic was tiny dust motes, riding the wind. I only noticed the sparkle of them when the light was gone."

"Dust motes?" he asked.

"They worked by touching skin, or being breathed in." She shuddered at the thought of how much she must have breathed in before she realized. "I followed them here, and found the source. It's a crystal inside that box."

"You tried to smash it?" He frowned, as if remembering her asking him to throw the rock into the box.

"Yes. But there was some magical barrier around it. And it came right at us when it realized we were trying to destroy it."

She saw some sparkles edging out from the bottom of the box. Forced herself to stand. "Cover your mouth and nose," she said, tossing him back his handkerchief and raising her own back over her mouth and nose.

She scooped up the rock again and crouched down beside the box. A moment later, Theo was beside her, thigh and shoulder touching, his lower face covered. With a deep breath, she flicked the box away and smashed the rock down.

She heard a crack.

She smashed the rock down again, and this time when she looked, she thought the glow was dimmer. When she lifted the rock and brought it down a third time, the light winked out.

The sparkles that had landed in thick layers on her gloves still shone, and she carefully reached out to grab the box and wiped them off into it.

The rest of the sparkles were black specks of soot, but there was at least a handful of active magic dust left.

She untied the handkerchief around her neck and laid it out, tipping the sparkles into the middle and then tying the four corners into a knot.

"Turnabout is fair play," she said, as she caught Theo's interested gaze. "We can use it on Marchant, if we get the chance."

Theo rose to his feet and reached down to help her up. But the look in his eye was less focused again, and she guessed the sparkles that had swirled up right at the end had found their mark.

When they were standing side by side, far closer than was

polite, his gaze fixed to hers. "I don't remember much of the afternoon."

"Me, either. The wind was blowing in our faces. We were breathing this in." She raised the kerchief and gave it a little shake.

He shuddered. "I kept meaning to slow down and wait for you, but I kept forgetting."

She acknowledged that with a nod. "Where are the others?"

He had to really think about it, spinning around as if to orientate himself. Finally he pointed upward. "On the hill above. Waiting for us." He shook himself, lifting his shoulders as if to shrug off the confusion completely.

"Let's go up the hill then." She didn't know why, but she held out her hand to him, and he took it immediately. She ducked beneath the crossed tree trunks and led the way back to her horse.

She could feel his hand get firmer in hers, less pliable, and eventually he tugged her to a stop, his grip tightening. "Where are we?"

She turned to face him. "We're in the forest."

He tilted his head. "It worries me that I can't remember."

"It'll come back to you. There was a magical trap." She held up the handkerchief. "What's left of it is in here."

"Magic trap." He repeated the words slowly. Then sucked in a breath. "We left you behind. I even thought how stupid that was, when we knew there could be traps. And then we left you behind."

He seemed so upset about it, she soothed him with a hand down his arm. "I think you did it because of the magic sparkles. They were blowing westward, and they probably reached us before we even got to the forest."

"Did he know we were coming?" Theo suddenly looked more focused, more alert, and his hand went to his sword.

"Given the debris around the box, I think he set this trap a long time ago. It was dependent on wind direction, and my guess is that he wants most people who arrive in Warven to be slightly befuddled. And those who take the quicker path through the forest to be more than just a little befuddled." There was some benefit to him, or he wouldn't do it, but she struggled to imagine how confusing everyone who came to Warven made sense. Maybe he liked them slightly disengaged, because it lowered inhibitions, and people might be more forthcoming about what they had with them, and why they were on the road.

She blushed. It had certainly lowered her inhibitions.

Theo tilted his head, looking at her, and he released his sword. "Never again, Melodie. I will have you in sight the rest of our journey."

He blinked suddenly, as if he had just remembered something. "Did I hold you? When I found you in the clearing?"

She blushed again. "We held each other," she said.

He gave a slow nod, as if it was all coming back to him. "I know why I did it," he said. "Why did you?"

She hesitated. "It felt good," she said, and then, from behind her, she heard her horse whinny, and she turned toward it in relief, jumping over the little stream.

"I think this is the same stream where we're camped above." Theo jumped after her and looked up the hill. He shook his head as if clearing it. "I feel like I'm waking up from a dream," he said. "Do I remember swirling embers and throwing a rock?"

"Yes," she said. "We smashed it in the end. But it fought us. That's why we lay down for a while, in a sort of dream. It was trying to stop us destroying it."

"I remember." He glanced at her, and suddenly grinned. "You are all pink-cheeked."

She blushed even more. Shook her head, but as she reached for her horse, he gently grabbed her shoulder, forced her to face him.

"I'm sorry I left you behind."

She made herself look in his eyes. "It wasn't you, it was the magic."

"It might have partly been the magic, but I was very focused on getting to Warven, and I should have been more careful with you." He glanced at the little sack of magic she held. "After all, this is the second time you've saved me."

"That's why you brought me along." She liked saying it.

"Yes. That is why I brought you along. This is just a very nice benefit."

Before she could ask him what was a very nice benefit, he pulled her even closer and kissed her cheek.

"What was that for?" she whispered, just as he had asked her when she had kissed his.

"For your great magic detecting abilities." He kissed her other cheek, in the Cervantes way, and then gently brushed his lips over her mouth.

She had been cloistered away, blocked from socializing, and given too much work. But she had seen the Cervantes and Kassian travelers as well as their military. They were respectful but confident with the people they were attracted to and had a healthy respect for boundaries.

Theo had the same feel about him. A deep sense of self, of his value.

She envied him.

She felt her cheeks heat until she wondered they didn't light the air around them.

"What is it?" he asked her, not letting go, but easing back and loosening his hold, so she could pull away if she wanted to.

She did not.

She forced her gaze upward. "Nothing."

"Good. Any time you want to stop, just say." He kissed her again, and then she was pushed forward, as her horse butted her back with its forehead.

Theo caught her, swinging her to the side and holding her around her shoulders and waist.

She looked up at him, wide-eyed.

He held her as if she was light as air.

If he had dropped her at that moment, it would have been fitting, because she felt as if she fell.

Instead, he lifted her easily back on her feet. "I think your horse wants its dinner."

She turned away. "So do I."

He took the reins from her and ran a large, calloused hand down her back. "I haven't looked after you very well. But I'll make it up to you."

She hoped he couldn't see the flush on her cheeks as she strode ahead, because even cloistered, her mind had gone places when he said that.

She was looking forward to how he intended to fulfill his promise.

CHAPTER 16

The others were gone.

Theo crouched beside the little fire pit he'd built before walking down the hill to fetch Melodie, and touched the stones.

Still warm.

For a moment, he wondered if the others had, under the grip of befuddlement, continued on to Warven. Given the heat in the stones, they were here as recently as an hour ago.

Melodie stood beside him, looking over the scene, and then walked past him to the stream. She came back with two horses, his own and Caro's.

"They were loose. I don't think he could take all of them, or maybe he already has too many, so he left these two free to go their own way. He probably hopes someone will find them and think themselves lucky."

"You think he took the team?" Theo had thought things would be difficult, but he had not suspected he would be bested before they even arrived in Warven.

"Yes." Melodie patted a horse's neck. "Maybe he checks here regularly, to see who has been caught in his confusion trap."

If that was so, it could be that persuading people off the road was part of the trap's magic. And he'd been in such a rush, he'd accepted Gallain's word without a murmur.

"Can you see if he was here? If he worked magic?" It was time he started using her expertise.

She hesitated, then gave a nod. "There isn't any magic to see anymore, but if someone uses it, I can sense . . . something. Like the smell in the air after it rains."

"He can't take every traveler he finds up here. Not if the trap's constantly putting out magic." Theo couldn't see how that would be feasible.

"No. But maybe he listened to them talking for a while before he struck, and heard something that made him realize they were here for the children."

That made sense.

Their enemy was forewarned.

"Then he knows about the two of us," he said.

"Maybe, maybe not." Melodie shrugged. "But it's best we assume he does." She bent and began picking up the things the others had left behind. Caro's bag, Ivan's cloak, two cups and the small kettle Theo had put on the fire to boil water.

She packed them into the saddle bag of Caro's horse.

"We need a story," she said.

She was pale, and he remembered she'd been looking forward to resting and a meal, but they couldn't stay here. Not in a place that Marchant checked regularly.

"A story for where?"

"The inn in Warven. We can't go on without sleep, but we can't stay here." She gently took her horse's reins from him, handed him his own, and began walking up the trail. "At least in Warven, with other people around, we can't disappear so easily. And there will be a door we can lock at a room in the inn. If we have a good enough story, we won't raise suspicion, and we can maybe gather some information about him."

"You've done this before," he said.

"I made a lot of enemies in my life," she said, glancing behind him. "Especially when I was much younger and innocently spoke about what I could see in a voice that was as clear and carrying as a bell, according to my father."

He smiled at the thought of a tiny Melodie, piping up in a sweet voice about the spell work she could see. He realized her father had probably been in constant fear of her being taken or silenced.

No wonder she had an air of loneliness about her. An aura of isolation.

He moved up, so they were walking side by side, the horses following behind. "We could present ourselves as a couple," he said. "So that sharing a room is a given."

She glanced at him, gave a serious nod. "Yes. I think that's a good idea."

"I don't want you out of my sight again. We're a team. We have my sword and the truth you can see when it comes to magic. Together, we have a better chance of protecting ourselves." He slipped an arm around her shoulder as they crested the hill, and saw Warven winking its lights at them below. Forests stretched along the hill to the left and right, but someone had cut a swathe through the trees wide enough for four horses abreast, all the way down to the bottom.

With night having fallen, the forests were an impenetrable wall of darkness, and something about it made the hair on the back of his neck stand on end.

He bent close to her ear. "We should also be aware he could be watching us right now."

She stiffened for a moment beneath his arm, and gave a nod. "Good point." She swept her gaze around, as if looking for a sign of their enemy, then leaned in close to him. "And we need to remember that everyone in Warven could be either under his spell, or a paid informant."

He gave a nod. That *was* worth keeping front of mind.

The path that led them downward twisted and turned, but was wide and well kept. Maybe Gallain wasn't under a spell when he'd suggested they take it.

"We should find the main road, and pretend we came in on it," he said.

She gave a nod. "And we'll have to pretend to be coming from Taunen, not Illoa."

With their story more or less straight, they reached the bottom of the hill and emerged onto the main road.

Warven was just ahead, the road open but empty. There was no gatehouse, which wasn't unusual in either Grimwalt or Kassia, where the government was stable and law and order was respected.

Someone did step out of the shadows where the road turned into the main street, though.

"Help you?" He was dressed like a town guard, in a tunic with a leather vest, leather arm braces and sturdy boots. A half-blade hung from his belt, but his hands were relaxed at his sides.

"Please," Theo said, easily. "We're looking for the inn."

"You're late on the road." The man indicated they follow him.

"We misjudged our timing, but we could see the lights every now and then on the road, and decided it would be better to push through than make camp so close to town."

The man drew in a deep breath. "Misjudging timing is common around these parts, but it feels like the wind has changed."

Theo felt Melodie tense by his side.

"The air does feel fresher," she said. "I feel like I've had a headache all day, but I think it's just the exhaustion speaking."

The man gave her a quick backward glance. "If you've been on the road all day, I'm not surprised." He gestured ahead of him, to a building with the lower floor lit up, and a few lights on in the story above. "The Warven Inn. Should have a room for you, and place for your mounts."

"Thank you." Theo watched as the man sauntered away, disappearing into the dark.

Neither of them spoke about him, or what he'd said, until they had the horses stabled, and were sitting in a warm corner of the inn with two steaming bowls of stew and a half loaf of bread between them.

"Not even here, I think," Melodie said, and he forced himself not to look behind him, to whoever her eyes had flicked to and then away from before she began to eat.

He threw himself into eating, as well, and enjoyed the way the small nook they'd settled into crammed them so close together. He would usually feel a little crowded and uncomfortable, but instead he just felt happy.

When they were finished, the innkeeper came to fetch their bowls herself.

"It's a good wind you blew in on," she said. "This is the first night we haven't had raised voices in I don't know how long." She stacked the bowls and grabbed up their mugs. "I had the boys warm water for a bath for you," she said, nodding to Melodie. "I know someone who's saddlesore when I see them."

Melodie gave a wincing smile. "Thank you. I might have difficulty just getting up from my seat, I'm so stiff."

The innkeeper gave a chuckle. "I'm Peg Hanson, but everyone just calls me Peggy. I spent some time in the saddle, but I'm very glad to be in one place, and off a horse these days."

She whisked away at a call from the bar, and Theo reached out and helped Melodie out of her seat. "Do you want to be carried upstairs?"

She gave another delightful blush and shook her head. "Maybe an arm to lean on, though."

He held out his arm, and she tucked her hand in the crook of his elbow.

They had adjusted his clothing on the road in to Warven to make him look less like someone in the military, and had invented a story of journeying to Illoa from Taunen, but there were still curious eyes on them as they made their way out of the tap room toward the stairs.

Everyone here was a potential enemy, and Theo let his gaze sweep the room as casually as he could before he helped Melodie up the stairs.

A man stared at him from a table, a mug of ale in front of him.

Theo nodded to him politely, and after a moment's surprised pause, the man nodded back.

If he could, Theo would hold a sword to each of their throats and frighten the truth from them, but they were alone here, with no help and no idea of who they were dealing with.

They would have to tread carefully.

CHAPTER 17

Melodie woke slowly, in the golden glow of sunrise. She could feel the light on her face, and the sounds of a busy inn outside the window. She sensed Theo lying next to her, the bed dipping a little toward him, and she realized she felt safe and comfortable.

She stretched and winced a little at the stiffness in her muscles, and then remembered how she'd crawled into bed after her bath and fallen asleep immediately, leaving Theo to worry about securing the room.

She winced as she looked to her right and found him awake, too, staring up at the ceiling with his hands folded beneath his head.

His arms were fascinating. He was shirtless and she could see the smooth golden skin and bunched muscles of his biceps, and she felt a familiar heating of her cheeks.

She really needed to keep her blushes under control.

She rolled on her side, toward him, and he looked over at her, his face so serious.

"You got some sleep?" she asked softly, suddenly worried he'd stayed up all night to watch her.

"I got plenty of sleep." His gaze flicked to the door, and she saw he had wedged a chair under the handle. The key was on the wooden dresser on the far side of the room. He lowered his voice. "No one bothered us."

"I'm sorry I left you to it," she said.

He put a finger to his lips and put his hand on the wall behind them, and finally, now she was concentrating, she heard the faintest shift of sound coming from the wall—a rustle of clothing.

"You hungry?" he asked suddenly, sitting up and turning to put his feet on the floor. "Because I'm starving."

"I'm hungry, and I'm pleased at the idea of not eating travel food," she answered.

"I'll go down, see if I can have something brought up here," he said, moving away from her, back still turned. She could see the definition of muscles in his back and on his shoulders. He wore soft, loose cotton pants that hung low on his hips. His clothes were draped over a chair set beside the fireplace, and he grabbed his trousers.

She caught just the smallest glimpse of him in profile, and then turned to give him privacy as he dressed, so glad she had an excuse to keep her face tilted away from him, because her cheeks were pink once again.

He was aroused.

She aroused him.

She was so delighted by the idea, she found herself smiling.

"Anything in particular you feel like for breakfast?" he asked, pulling his shirt over his head.

She lifted up a little on her elbows, letting him see the gleam in her eye and the fluster on her face. "Anything they have is good."

He stared at her, rooted to the spot, and then shook his head, as if to clear it. "Got it." He opened the door.

"Theo," she called.

He paused in the doorway. "Yes."

"Your boots."

He looked down at his bare feet and shook his head again. Pointed a finger at her as if to say that was her fault.

She giggled, then slapped a hand over her mouth.

Had she ever giggled?

Maybe, when she was little. When it was just her and her father, and they had been somewhere safe.

He walked back, sat down and pulled on socks and boots in the quick, economical movements of a soldier, then left, locking the door behind him.

As soon as he was gone, she remembered the listener at the wall, and her breathing sped up.

Was it just another guest, sitting up against their pillows and making a noise they weren't aware of? Or was someone trying to spy on them?

She had to assume it was a spy.

She got up, found her bag, and walked behind the neck-high screen Peggy had put up around the bathtub. She changed out of the cotton pants and tunic she had slept in, into thick trousers, a clean shirt and her usual boots.

There was a quick, single knock at the door and then Theo unlocked it and stood in the doorway, his eyes widening a little at the sight of her behind the screen.

"It'll be easier to go down," he said. "They're so busy in the tap room, the food will be cold by the time they bring it up."

"I'm ready." She stepped out, and her gaze went back to the wall. "How many visitors are staying at the inn? I know I was probably told last night, but I don't remember."

"You were pretty tired." Theo stepped back into the hallway, and his gaze flicked to the door next to theirs. "There was a traveler who left early this morning, so it's just ourselves and someone who came in even later than we did." He tilted his head to the left, indicating the room next door. "Peggy says they're headed to Illoa, too."

"So all the patrons they're dealing with downstairs are locals, then?" she asked, walking past him so he could lock up behind her.

"Must be," Theo agreed. His gaze flicked again to the door beside theirs, and then he held out an arm for her to take as they reached the stairs.

She smiled as she took it. "I'm not quite so decrepit this morning as I was last night. Although I'm still stiff."

"I like your hand on my arm," he said simply.

She tightened her grip, and he reached over to brush his fingers over her wrist before they took the stairs.

It *was* packed in the tap room, but Peggy had kept their little nook for them—probably the benefit of being an actual guest of the inn— and as soon as they had taken a seat, she plied them with food and hot tea.

They had just started to eat when a man came down the stairs. He looked prosperous, and slightly thickset, but his eyes were small and dark, darting toward them as soon as he reached the tap room, and then away to where Peggy was dealing with customers at the bar.

He turned away from them and went to speak to Peggy, then followed her over to them.

Melodie could guess what was coming. There was no other table to sit at.

"Do you mind sharing the table with a fellow guest?" Peggy asked, and one of her workers brought a third chair over. "This is Kandra Gus."

"Not at all." Theo smiled, friendly and affable.

She needed to be the same.

After they'd introduced themselves, Kandra Gus sat down and they waited politely until he had food and drink himself before they continued eating their own.

"Peggy told me you're headed for Illoa," Gus said.

Melodie sent him a beaming smile, and wondered if he was the magic user they were looking for. Theo didn't have a clear memory of what he looked like, but whoever it was would know Theo. He had spelled him into a goat, after all. If Kandra Gus was their enemy, he would know they were lying no matter what she said, so she didn't worry about it.

"Eventually," she said.

"Oh, I thought you were on your way today?" Gus paused with a spoonful of scrambled eggs on his fork.

"Theo promised me some time out of the saddle." Melodie sent the same sunny smile to Theo, and he returned it like a love-sick swain. "I can barely move. So we're resting today and tomorrow, at least, just to get the use of my muscles back."

"I see." Gus looked between them. "Haven't you been traveling from Taunen? I think that's what Peggy told me?"

In other words, haven't you already had a lot of time in the saddle? Melodie thought. It was a good question.

She smiled again. "Our cart overturned and broke. Unfixable." She lifted her shoulders sadly. "We had to sell so much of our stock in the small village where it happened, because we obviously couldn't transport it, but we were so looking forward to seeing Illoa, we decided to press on anyway. But I'd forgotten how long it's been since I was in a saddle instead of sitting on a cart bench. I'm reminded now, though." She gave a wince as she shifted in her chair. "Brutal."

"Are you headed off today?" Theo asked him politely. "And are you traveling on from Illoa into Kassia?"

"I have some business in Warven, so it depends how long it takes me to get it done." Gus scraped the last food off his plate. "I might see you tonight, or I might not."

"Well, happy travels." Melodie smiled at him, taking a slow, unhurried sip of her tea.

He gave a nod, pushed his chair back, pulled something out of his pocket, and threw it at Theo.

It lifted up, a golden net so gossamer light it floated upward on an air current and hovered, suspended for a moment. Melodie jumped up, leaped onto her chair, got her hand above it, and shoved it back down at Kandra Gus.

He stared at her, slacked-jawed, and she realized he didn't know what she had done. Perhaps couldn't even see what he'd thrown at Theo very well. When it floated down and settled on his head, he sat back down on his chair in a slump.

"Melodie." Theo stood, angling out of the nook and putting a hand on Kandra Gus's shoulder to stop him getting up.

"It's all right." She kept her voice soft. "He's not going anywhere. Question is, does he have a helper, because if that had landed on you, how would he have taken us both?"

"Had what landed on me?" Theo's gaze swept the tap room.

"The net." Melodie inched out herself. "See anyone suspicious?"

"Maybe." His gaze locked on someone close to the side door, and as Melodie got free of the table, she caught the back view of a woman, pushing the doors open and escaping outside.

"I'll get her. Can you bring him with you to the stables?" Theo was already moving.

"Yes." Melodie was careful not to touch the net. "Come now, Gus, let's go outside. Follow me."

He stood compliantly and did exactly as she asked. The crowd had thinned since the breakfast rush and it was easy enough to take the exit closest to the stables.

As they walked to the door, she checked the patrons to see if they were watching the drama, but either no one had been looking their way, or they didn't think it that strange.

Once they'd made it outside, she blinked against the brightness of the sun. Despite the cloudless day, the air was cool, and she shivered a little after the warmth of the inn. She needed her jacket or at least a vest over her shirt.

Gus stumbled on the uneven cobbles, and she took his arm, leading him to the large, well-built stables set along the side of the inn.

"Here." Theo's voice came from around the corner of the building, and Melodie steered Gus along with her, and found Theo holding a woman up against the back wall, completely out of sight of the courtyard between the stables and the inn.

"So, you and Kandra Gus are a team?" Melodie said. "What's your name?"

The woman was thin, wiry, and older than Melodie had originally thought. About the same age as Gus himself. The clothes she wore looked a little more worn than Gus's and she looked less sleek and prosperous.

"Name's Nena, and we're not a team." The woman spat to the side. "He pays me, and tries to undercut the final amount. That's how things work between us."

"And what was he paying you to do today?" Theo asked.

"To grab her." Nena nodded to Melodie. "He said he would have you under control, and would lead you outside, and I was to bring the woman along, and pretend like we were going to help you." She lifted one shoulder. "Looks like you managed to turn the tables on him."

"Looks like," Melodie agreed.

There was a beat of silence, and Nena's eyes moved from Gus to Theo to her, and she looked frightened.

"I know he meant you harm. I'm not stupid. But he pays me, and I need the money. I know you got no cause to feel friendly toward me, but if I tell you what I know, will you let me go?"

"Depends if, after you tell us what you know, we believe you." Theo sounded as grim as an executioner.

Nena hesitated, then gave a nod, her eyes sliding over and over to Gus, as if she couldn't believe his demeanor.

He stood, smiling slightly, swaying a little in place, but otherwise completely placid.

"Gus here comes through Warven at least twice a month, sometimes more. I live just outside town, and he's used me a few times to help him." Her eyes darted away, and Melodie wondered what that help had entailed. "He takes his orders from someone who lives nearby, and he comes and goes between Taunen and Illoa, and sometimes even further, for whoever it is he works for. He buys things or collects things, and drops them off. And every now and then, he does something a little more hands on than just delivering packages."

"Like this time," Theo said.

She gave a nod. "He arrived very late last night, to tell me to be at the inn early, and I was to have breakfast in the tap room and wait for him to give me the signal."

"Where would you have taken us?" Melodie asked.

"I don't know. I've never been to the big boss's house," she said. "Gus calls him Marchant. He lives down the road from me. At least, I think he does. But then, this place was always a little muddled, you know? I've felt more myself since yesterday evening than I have for a while." Nena rubbed at her arms. "A lot of people are feeling that. I heard the talk this morning in the tap room."

"How long have you had this arrangement with Kandra Gus?" Melodie asked.

"Three years," she said, and there was a depth of bitterness to her voice that told Melodie she had hated every minute of those years.

"He short-changes you, you said?" Theo asked.

"Yes, but it's not just that . . ."

"You don't like the work," Melodie said. "So why did you do it?"

Nena looked down. "I just haven't been able to think straight for the last few years. Everything just stopped working for me on my smallholding. There's something wrong with me. I keep forgetting what I need to do, and things went to ruin. Gus offered me a way to keep myself from having to sell up."

Melodie felt a little spike of excitement. "Where is your place?"

"Just outside of town, up into the forest a little way, to the right." She pointed over the field that was fenced off behind the stables, toward the woods. "It's a road that leads nowhere. Maybe it used to be a shortcut to Skäddar, but it wasn't maintained, and now it's quicker to take the Taunen road and then branch off further to the north." She waved in a north westerly direction. Put her arm down. "So, can I go?"

Theo released her. "Yes."

She stepped away, unsure if they meant it, but when neither of them made any move toward her, she gave a dip of her head and ducked around the corner. Melodie could hear her boots jogging away on the cobbles.

"What's wrong with him?" Theo asked, jerking his chin at Gus.

"He tried to throw a net of compliance over you. I tossed it back over him." Melodie turned her attention to Gus. "He'll do whatever we ask."

Theo studied Gus, and Melodie saw the horror on his face. "That would have been me?"

She nodded. "He will answer truthfully, though. Which is good, because Marchant obviously knows who we are, or very clearly suspects us, or he wouldn't have sent these two to grab us. That net is magically valuable. I've only seen something like it once in my life before."

"But it's gone wrong for him." There was satisfaction in Theo's voice. "We have Gus. And the net."

She nodded.

Gus started walking to the fence, and Melodie gently grabbed him by the arm and led him back. "Lean against the stable wall and enjoy the sun," she told him, and he did it with a smile.

"So, who do you work for?" Theo asked him, leaning against the wall beside him.

If anyone came around the corner, they'd look like three weary travelers, enjoying the sunshine and the green fields.

"Marchant," he whispered, then tapped the side of his nose. "I've never seen his face." Gus turned his hand palm up. "He always meets me just past Nena's farm, and he wears a covering over his face, a hat, and long, flowing clothes."

Probably less to hide his face and more because the confusion spell blew in that direction when the wind was right, Melodie guessed. And their man couldn't afford to ever have a foggy thought.

"You've never seen him?" Melodie was skeptical. "How did he come to hire you?"

"I was boasting a little in the inn on my way through a couple of years ago. Went on my way the next day, and he came up to me when I was sitting around my camp fire on the way to Taunen."

"Covered up?" Theo asked.

"Maybe." Gus shrugged. "He kept behind me, touching my neck with the tip of a knife. Told me he'd pay me well, but he expected quick service and no lies." He shrugged again. "He *has* paid me well. It's been a good deal."

"So when he says go throw a net of compliance over someone in the inn, you do it?" Theo asked.

"I was a bit nervous today, truth be told." Gus looked more awake than he had since the conversation began. "Usually you won't believe what I can get away with here, because everyone's wandering around half-asleep. But today, everyone was so clear-eyed."

"So, being so aware and clear-eyed, we turned the tables on you." Melodie liked that he'd come up with his own story about how they'd bested him. "What happens now?"

"I'll have to go tell him I failed." Gus slumped against the wall, back bent, head bowed.

"It's okay," Melodie consoled him. "It wasn't your fault that everyone is more awake now."

"That's true." Gus gave a grateful nod. "I could tell last night already, and it was only more obvious this morning. I've never seen the tap room so lively and so full."

"When did your boss tell you to watch us?" Theo asked.

"He hires a man to watch the road into town." Gus waved a hand the way they'd come in the night before. "He said two people came in with very good horses."

"You were nearby?" Melodie asked. She was impressed if Marchant had a way to contact Gus from afar.

"I always go straight to the meeting spot, just past Nena's place, when I have a new delivery, like I did yesterday. I ring the bell he leaves there. It has to be magical because he wouldn't be able to hear it, otherwise. If he doesn't come after about a half hour or so, I leave whatever I have for him in a box to the side."

"But he came last night?" Theo asked.

"He was already there. I passed the watchman on my way.

Marchant told me to get Nena to help me, and to grab you both, and deliver you tonight."

"You think it's a half hour walk for him from his house to the clearing?" Melodie asked.

"That's the usual time." Gus shrugged. "Sometimes longer, but never less."

"Well, Gus, what you're going to do now is go back to your room and have a good rest. We'll call you when it's time to go ring the bell."

"A rest?" Gus's eyes teared up. "That would be nice."

They walked back to the inn with Gus, let him go up the stairs before they did, and then followed him up.

He was standing looking at the door, as if trying to work out how to open it.

"Do you have the key?" Melodie asked.

He dug in his pocket and pulled it out, showed it to her.

Theo took it from him, unlocked the door, and nudged him in. "Go lie down and rest."

Then Theo locked the door behind him and slid the key into his own pocket.

"What now?" Melodie asked.

Theo couldn't leash his excitement. "Now we do some reconnaissance."

CHAPTER 18

Viviane was the daughter of the queen of Kassia and the Commander of the Cervantes, and she knew a soldier from her parents' army when she saw one.

And she saw four.

It made her heart skitter in her chest.

"Who are they?" Genevieve whispered. The two of them were lying, heads together, on the bench against the wall, and they had a clear view of the four soldiers chained to the wall in the antechamber outside their cell. The moonlight was just enough to illuminate them.

"I don't know them, but they're from Kassia and Cervantes."

The quiet sound of a shoe on the flagstone floor had her lifting her head. Jon was crouched near them, as far as his chain would allow, his gaze focused on their would-be rescuers.

"They're looking for us," he breathed. "Everyone is looking for us."

"Of course they are," Vivi replied, but she felt the same relief she heard in his voice.

She had wondered how anyone would find them. But somehow, they were at least looking in the right direction.

"Did he enspell them, like he did with us?" Gen asked.

Vivi nodded. "How else would he take four trained soldiers from our army?" Her father made sure all his warriors were as good as they could be.

She thought their abductor had been badly injured sometime after they'd been taken, or he had a long term injury that had flared up. She hadn't remembered him moving as if he were in pain on the night he'd taken them, but now he did—slow, tentative steps, and he had difficulty bending down.

Spell work was the only way he could have taken four warriors.

It eased her heart a little that these soldiers had been taken, just like she and her friends had been. They were older, stronger. More experienced.

Another rustle of clothing from the dark corner of their cell told Vivi that Ric was coming to join them. He had recovered the slowest of them all, and she still suspected their abductor had hurt him, not just put him into a magical sleep.

She'd kept a close eye on him since they'd begun moving around and felt more themselves, but he was slower, and moved like he hurt. Just like their abductor did.

He said he was fine, but she didn't believe him, and she didn't think Jon did either.

She slid off the bench and sat, leaning back against the hard wood, and covertly studied him.

He was chained further back than Jon, and ended up sitting cross-legged, his chain lifted off the ground and stretching behind him.

They sat in silence, but none of the four soldiers so much as stirred, and Vivi got a good idea of how things had been for her and her friends before they had finally woken, hungry, thirsty and stiff.

Their abductor came every morning with two jugs of water, a loaf of bread, four apples and a hunk of cheese, and they had to ration it how they saw fit through the day.

It was better that way, she had decided after the first day.

When he turned his attention to them more fully, things would be far, far worse. Of that, she was positive.

There was a glee in his voice and on his face when he opened the grate to one side to push the food and water through, and take the empty platter from the day before. Sometimes he set the platter and jugs just inside, and as the one chained closest, Vivi had to stretch out on her stomach to reach them.

At least there were two latrines built into the cell, one in each of the back corners. They were nothing but two overlapping brick walls set in the corner that shielded a hole in the ground. All of the chains were just long enough to allow them inside.

At least it gave a modicum of privacy, but Vivi had the feeling that they would have no secrets from each other by the time they got out of here.

And they would.

They would get out of here.

CHAPTER 19

Nena's smallholding looked as rundown and dilapidated as she'd said it was.

She was a victim, Theo reminded himself. While she'd been explaining her inability to work, he'd recalled his own strange feelings of befuddlement, and he had only been exposed to it for a few hours. She lived on the edge of the spell, and when the wind blew her way, she would have had no escape from a blight she couldn't see.

He and Melodie were on foot, and it had taken them twenty minutes to reach the broken gate into Nena's property from the inn, the road curving gently up the hill, but winding to the right side.

He'd stopped to look down the rutted path that led to her house, hidden by a line of trees with just the roofline visible, but Melodie grabbed his arm as he turned to walk on, toward Gus's meeting spot, her grip strong enough to surprise him.

"Stop."

He froze, allowing her to pull him right up against her.

"What is it?" he breathed the word into her ear.

"A spell." She drew him through the gate, toward Nena's

house, and then off the drive, walking along the broken fence line, so they were still moving parallel to the road, over rough ground.

"Here." She pointed to a spot on the track that was in line with the only pole that wasn't rotting away.

He saw another pole on the opposite side of the road. "A trip wire?" he asked.

"Something that looks a bit like a spider's web," she said. "Might be that it even feels like one when you touch it."

A warning system.

Theo didn't like the fact that he couldn't see the danger around him. He was blind in this fight.

"It looks as if he's set it up to give him a warning every time someone comes down the road. Kandra Gus must set it off each time." Melodie put her hands on the fence, looking back at the web, and Theo boosted her over it.

She sent him a quick look he found difficult to read, and then he vaulted over the fence to join her on the road.

"Gus said it takes Marchant about half an hour to get to the meeting place after he rings the bell, but either it takes longer than that, because instead of coming when he hears the bell, he leaves as soon as Gus activates the warning web, or it doesn't take Marchant long to get there, but he doesn't show himself immediately, and lies in wait to make sure Gus hasn't double-crossed him." Theo stared at the road, seeing nothing, although he did notice both poles holding the magical web were new. That was something to look out for. Marchant maintained what was useful to him, but left everything else. The new poles were stark against the rotting wood of the others.

"He's cautious," Melodie said. "Almost paranoid."

"This is a man who turned me into a goat rather than juggle me and the children." Theo shook his head. "Cautious doesn't begin to describe it."

"He's afraid." Melodie crouched down, although she didn't get any closer to the web, and looked from one side of the road to the other. "He eliminates all risk to himself, as much as possible. He's a coward."

That rang true. The problem was, cowards were usually the most dangerous adversaries, in Theo's experience.

"What are you looking for?" Theo couldn't see anything at all, and he felt on edge. Every rustle of the bushes that lined the road, every bird call, suddenly seemed full of menace.

"I'm trying to see how he's alerted when the web is broken." She moved to the middle of the road and looked over her shoulder at him, then crouched down again, lay on her back, head toward the invisible web, and wriggled toward it.

Her hair caught under her, and she stopped, grabbed it in a hand, twisted it and lay it over her shoulder, then carefully continued moving back.

He said nothing, leaving her to concentrate, but he drew his sword. He could do nothing to help her, but he could make sure she was safe.

After a few minutes, she wiggled back, and her shirt rode up on her stomach, showing him a smooth, bared midriff.

He slid his sword back in its scabbard and extended his hand. She reached up to him so he could lift her back to her feet. "What did you find?"

She made a sound of exasperation as she tucked her shirt back in. "I didn't find anything. Maybe there's a second item linked to this trap that he keeps close. It could react in some way when the web is touched. I can't see anything that would fly or travel to warn him."

"He has a lot of tricks," Theo said. "The rope to turn me into a goat. The net he gave to Gus. This web. The spell in the forest."

"If what Kandra Gus says is true, he collects things." She stopped suddenly. "Like me."

"What have you collected?" Theo frowned.

"Lots of things, through the years. If they're dangerous, I burn them. And the benign magical items I find, I put in the hands of people I think can best use them. But there are a few I've kept. A protection bead that I worked into this ring."

She held it up. "It's how I was able to break free from the confusion trap in the forest yesterday, at least enough to go looking for it."

Theo took her hand, studied the ring. It was made of rose gold and the design was a simple flower, with rose gold petals and a smooth, pink quartz bead in the middle. It looked inexpensive, but if this ring could warn its wearer of danger, he knew it was worth a fortune.

"I'm glad you had it," he said. He and Melodie would most likely also be prisoners without it.

"I have a silver brooch, too. But the magic in that is weak, and I can't see what it does. It may be the magic is so depleted, it isn't possible to tell, so I've kept it to be cautious. And I have a book of health remedies. I only found it last month, and I haven't found the right person to give it to," she said. Then she lifted a shoulder. "I also have a handkerchief that has protective magic woven into it, but it's for a very specific person, so it is useless to anyone else. It reminds me of someone who saved me long ago, so I've kept it for sentimental reasons."

"So this man can see spell work like you, do you think?" Theo said. "And has chosen to make it his livelihood?"

"If he'd stuck to items, that would be one thing, although it seems he has dealt in very dark work. But he's taken people." Melodie drew in a breath. "People like himself. Like me." She shook her head. "My father's greatest fear was that someone would discover my ability and take me. People come to Grimwalt if they think their child has any magical talent because they think they'll be safer here, but this man *lives* in Grimwalt."

"And he was trawling for victims in Kassia and Cervantes." Theo wondered if he'd already cleared out the victims he could find around where he lived.

It was not a good thought.

"Do you think he took the children because they're magical, or because they had some magical items with them?" She frowned.

"He said to me . . ." Theo realized he had not told her exactly what had happened. Most of it had come back to him in short flashes, but since this morning, he thought he remembered everything. "He said I shone with talent, just like the children. He also appeared out of nowhere, so we need to understand he may well have a cloak of invisibility. And his hand . . ." He remembered the hand flung out at him, and couldn't remember whether Marchant held anything in it. But as he'd swung his sword, that hand seemed to flick something at him and all the air had been pulled from his lungs.

"What about his hand?" Melodie's own hand was still resting lightly in his from his inspection of her ring, and she turned it, grasping his hand to comfort him.

"He gestured to me and it felt like ice against my skin. Suddenly, I couldn't breathe."

Melodie stared at him, and there was fear in her eyes. "That is a lot of magical power for us to overcome."

"I should have told you this before I asked you to come along, but I only remembered all the details this morning."

"That's what you were thinking about this morning, staring up at the ceiling?" she asked.

"No. That wasn't what I was thinking about." He bent his head and brushed a kiss on her lips.

The sound of something scurrying in the thick hedge that bordered the road forced him to pull back, listening.

"My ring is quiet," Melodie told him.

He met her bright gaze, and gave a nod. "Let's hope it stays that way."

He forced his attention from her and focused on the world around him. It seemed to fade away when he got too close to her, but now was not the time to enjoy that.

But when this was done, he would. He most certainly would.

They walked for another ten minutes, until he saw a path through the hedge. Given the footprints visible in the soft sand, he guessed this was the way to the meeting spot.

He stopped on the road, waiting for Melodie to reach his side.

"See anything?" he asked.

"No. Let me go first, though."

He didn't want to let her, but right now, she could see the danger better than he could.

He gave a nod, keeping close behind her as she began down the path.

The hedge disappeared in a few steps, and they were suddenly in a gloomy clearing, surrounded by young growth trees, which filtered the light green.

There was the bell, sitting on a massive tree stump.

Melodie moved around it slowly. "The bell is magical," she said. "But that's the only thing that is, that I can see."

"I'm going to work my way through the trees," Theo told her. He wanted to see if Marchant had a place where he could stand and watch Gus before he made himself known.

He found the gap in the trees which seemed the most likely place to enter the clearing from the opposite side, and a few steps back he found a well-worn spot with a clear view of the clearing if you crouched down.

He watched Melodie walking around, and then she stopped. She closed her eyes and tilted her head back. He didn't know if she was listening for danger, or enjoying the cool green of the woods and the sound of birdsong and the babble of a nearby brook.

It was idyllic if you took away the reason they were here.

The light filtered through the leaves to touch her long dark hair, illuminating the golden strands within the dark brown, and gilding her beautiful face.

Suddenly, her eyes snapped open, and she turned, looking toward the road.

He was in the clearing as fast as he could move.

Her gaze met his, and she lifted a finger to her lips.

He stepped close to her, and pulled her even closer before he bent his lips to her ear. "Danger?"

She shook her head, then hesitated. "Not sure. Someone is coming, though."

He could hear them, too, now, coming toward them from the road.

With no good way out, and the possibility that someone was here to ring the bell, and draw Marchant to a meeting, he guided her with him between the trees, where he found a place to hide where Marchant, even if he crouched down in his hiding spot, wouldn't see them.

It was a tight fit with two of them, and she wound her arms around him, and he her, so they were tight up against each other.

"Gus? You here?"

It was Nena.

Had she seen them?

Or maybe she had caught a brief glimpse of them as they stepped off the track and down the path, and thought it must be Gus.

She stood, looking around, stared at the bell for a little while, and then backed away.

As she left, she was muttering under her breath.

"Wait," Theo whispered to Melodie as she started to pull away. "She might have triggered the web."

She gave a nod in response and they stood together in silence.

Eventually, Theo decided Nena must have come over the fence and bypassed the web. It was a lucky break.

But he gave it just a minute more before he reluctantly stepped away.

"All right?" he asked her, still in a whisper.

She pushed her forehead into his chest for a moment, looking down, then tipped her head to look at him. Gave a nod.

There was a lot he wanted to ask her, because there was all

kinds of things going on behind those eyes of hers, but now was most definitely not the time and place.

"Let's get back to the inn and get Gus," he said. "And put an end to this."

CHAPTER 20

She was worried about quite a few of the older warriors who rode with her in the tight group.

She glanced over at Luc, but he was focused ahead, face grim, feelings held close and tightly controlled.

She reached out, even as their horses galloped over uneven ground, and brushed her fingers lightly down his upper arm.

He turned his head, his gaze meeting hers, and she saw the rage burning in his eyes. It matched her own, but unlike in some—like Rafe—it was a clear rage.

Rafe worried her because this kidnap, this abduction, had him spiraling back to memories of the Chosen camps, and a few of his fellow officers along with him.

She flicked her gaze ahead, to where Rafe rode in front, and back to Luc, and he gave a nod, urging his mount ahead; allowing the advantage of rank as others let him through.

He caught up with his second-in-command, and forced his pace to slow.

Ava noticed a sigh of relief ripple through the unit at the slacking off of what had been an almost impossible pace.

Suddenly, from up ahead, someone called out a hail, and the whole riding party went stone-faced and ready for trouble, before the call came again, and from the suddenly relaxed postures, Ava guessed it was the correct hail from one of their own.

Luc and Rafe slowed their mounts to a walk, and then finally to a stop. They had cut across from Ta-lin to take the road north that ran some of the way along the Bartolo River, and the horses moved straight to the banks to drink, their sides heaving.

Both men dismounted as four soldiers came into view, looking like they'd be riding hard themselves. At the sight of their commander and his second-in-command, they snapped to attention and pulled up on the reins, then eased themselves from their saddles.

Ava thought they would have slid off, groaning, if they'd been alone.

They were clearly known to some of the soldiers in the group, because as everyone dismounted, there were greetings and some back-slapping, which made Ava think they'd been trained in Fernwell and Ta-lin.

She wondered if this was a coincidence, or if they had some news to share about Viviane, and where she was.

A soldier came to take her mount to the river to drink, and she murmured a word of thanks and then stepped forward so she was shoulder to shoulder with Luc, eager to find out why they were here.

"My queen." One of the riders obviously recognized her and bowed his head and put a fist to his heart, and the other three followed suit, shock at the sight of her etched on their faces.

This salute was something Luc had told her to stop fighting against. He had started it, so she blamed him for its entrenchment. Way back when the Rising Wave had first taken Fernwell and established control of Kassia, she had planned to divest herself of the title and move the country to a parliamentary system, like Grimwalt.

That had been harder than she'd thought it would be, and when it was discovered that Grimwalt's parliament had been corrupted by a spell worker, it had become even more difficult to shift the old ways.

Eventually, she had settled on a compromise. She wasn't exactly a figurehead, her word still carried weight, but she was no longer the only decision-maker in Kassia and Cervantes. The people had some say in their own fate.

"We were hoping to meet you on the road," one of the soldiers said.

"You're based in Illoa, aren't you, Tiano?" Gunnar, one of the older soldiers, asked, and the woman nodded.

"We were sent by our captain to help General Bardet if he needed assistance on his way to Ta-lin, and to bring news about developments."

"Theo was at your barracks?" Rafe asked.

Ava realized that was the only way they could know Rafe would be traveling this way.

Her breath hitched as she realized these soldiers had actual news.

Luc reached out and grabbed her hand, squeezed it gently, and she wondered if he was warning her not to expect too much.

"He was in Illoa, sir." Tiano turned to Rafe respectfully. "He rode into Grimwalt, following after the abductor, and Captain Draper gave him four soldiers to accompany him."

"Listen up." Luc raised his voice, cutting off the rising murmurs. "Everyone eat, drink, rest for a bit."

There were interested gazes that told Ava the other soldiers knew they were being excluded from a more in-depth debrief, but they also knew they'd find out eventually, so suddenly the unit of thirty scattered, the noise level increased, and the tension seemed to lessen.

"Let's talk," Luc said to Tiano. His gaze swept over the other three. "All of you."

He led them to the side, and Rafe and Lineka came with them.

Lineka's son Jonquil was one of the other abductees, and Ava shared a quick, hopeful look with him as they gathered around.

"Give us everything, Tiano. Including impressions. And if anyone has something different to say, you say it." Luc's order was implacable.

"Sir." Tiano stiffened at the order, face earnest. "Two nights ago, Lieutenant Hallan came into the barracks. He had no weapons and he looked terrible. He asked for the captain, and then after the captain finished speaking with him, she called us in. She said when we met up with you, you would want to know everything, and so she gave us information that we would not usually be high enough in rank to know."

"She was right," Luc said. "Keep going, soldier."

Tiano cleared her throat. "Lieutenant Hallan said he followed the abductor in the direction of Grimwalt, and found his camp. He saw the children, alive but bound, lying around the fire, and he circled them, looking for the abductor or abductors. Suddenly, a man was behind him, and the lieutenant told Captain Draper he thought perhaps he had been wearing something to make himself invisible, because he would have seen him earlier, otherwise."

Ava felt a shiver down her arms. She had worn something that made her invisible many times.

"He and the magic user fought, and as the lieutenant struck a blow, he said something was done to him. He was on the ground, unable to breathe. The man told him he was too much to handle, given he had the children as well, and then he remembered nothing more."

"So he escaped later?" Ava asked, and the shiver turned into a chill. The description of the children bound up had her hoping there was no magic rope involved in this. She felt nauseous at the thought of someone who was holding her precious baby, or any child, having something like what had been used on her long ago. Sucking away her life and her spirit.

"He . . ." Tiano looked at the other three, as if nervous about what she was going to say next.

"It doesn't matter what it is," Luc told her, voice gentle. "We need to hear it."

"It's just . . ." Tiano shrugged and blew out a breath. "Lieutenant Hallan says he was turned into a goat sometime after he was made unconscious." She hesitated, then plowed on. "But the lieutenant had hurt the abductor in the struggle and he thinks the man was unconscious or badly hurt. He was found by another trader on the road who was headed to the Illoa market on the Grimwalt side. For some reason, instead of keeping him, though, he tied him to the bridge, as a tribute to Malin."

Luc looked over at Ava, face slack with surprise. As if asking her if it was even possible.

"I've never heard of magic that can turn someone into something else, but that doesn't mean it doesn't exist." Ava's voice shook a little. This was someone who was powerful. She couldn't even conceive of doing magic like that.

"Continue," Luc said.

Tiano shook her shoulders. "While he was tied to the bridge in Illoa, on the Grimwalt side, a woman noticed him, rescued him, and freed him of the spell. That is how he was able to come to the barracks."

"What woman?" Every instinct in Ava came awake.

"Some Grimwaldian." Tiano shrugged, as if that was all the explanation necessary.

Grimwalt *did* have the highest concentration of magic users. Ava was Grimwaldian herself, as it happened.

"You don't know her name?" Luc asked, just managing to keep the impatience from his voice.

Ava knew him well enough to hear it though, just under the surface.

They all shook their heads.

"She came to the barracks later that same night, though," another of the soldiers said. "The lieutenant had asked her to help him find the abductor, and she agreed."

Tiano nodded. "The captain said the woman was going to leave in the morning with the rescue party. Because if they were up against a magic user, it would help to have someone with her skills along."

"Her skills?" Lineka spoke for the first time, his voice hoarse, as if he had been screaming.

"She could see the goat was enspelled. That's how she knew to rescue the lieutenant." Tiano lifted her hands. "I'm not sure of the details. But she, the lieutenant, and four soldiers from the barracks, left at daybreak," Tiano said.

"And they knew where to go?" Rafe asked.

"The woman who saved the lieutenant had interacted with the trader who'd tied him to the bridge before he left the city. She thought he may know where the spell worker was from, so they were going to catch up to him on the Taunen road and get more information, then take it from there."

There was a plan, at least, Ava thought. But that was a far cry from knowing where the children were, other than somewhere on the Taunen road.

Her heart physically ached with worry, with fear, and with stress.

And still, they had more information now than they'd had before. Much more.

It seemed for the first time, she was going up against someone as powerful, if not more powerful, than herself.

She only hoped that Viviane had managed to keep her own power hidden. Because having been locked away for years by someone who wanted to use her, Ava would fight until there was nothing left in her to save her daughter from the same fate.

CHAPTER 21

THE LEANER, slightly shorter of the two men woke up swearing.

Viviane had been watching the soldiers since the dawn light had begun to illuminate the room through the small window high on the wall above them.

The light hit her and Genevieve first, and then slowly moved back along the floor through the day until, just before midday, it shone directly in the soldier's face.

He looked rough, with dark stubble on his cheeks and rumpled clothes. But all four of them looked tough and competent.

Just having them in the holding cell had given her some comfort.

The man sat up with a hoarse shout, looked around, eyes wild, and then slumped back against the wall.

"Shit." He smacked the man beside him. "Ivan. Wake up."

Ivan came awake with a snort, and then, as his gaze met Viviane's, his eyes widened.

"Viviane?" he asked.

She gave a nod, although she wondered how he'd guessed who she was. She knew she looked like her mother, and every soldier in the army had met the queen at least once. "This is Jon, Genevieve, and Ricardo."

The woman who had been lying pressed up against Ivan came awake so suddenly, she seemed to go from prone to crouching in a moment.

"Fuck me," she breathed. "We were taken." She reached over and tapped the woman beside her on the cheek. "Jacinta."

Jacinta groaned, turned over, and the other woman smacked her on the shoulder. "Up."

Jacinta opened an eye, breathed in sharply, and sat up. "Shit."

"That's what I said." The man who'd woken first looked down at the shackle on his ankle, then back to the wall to see where it was attached.

"He had to double up," Viviane said.

Their abductor only had two attachments for chains on the wall opposite their cell, so he'd shackled the two men together, and the two women together at their ankles.

While she was talking, Genevieve had moved off the bench, extending her chain as far as she could, and sat down beside her, cross-legged on the ground. As soon as she did, the boys began to move across as well.

Jon suddenly frowned at the first man who'd woken. "I know you," he said. "You're Gallain."

Gallain narrowed his eyes, then knocked his head back against the wall softly. "I did guard duty in Ta-lin and your father was head of command. Captain Lineka."

This was good. Viviane felt a rush of relief. She hadn't exactly believed the arrival of the soldiers was a trick, but having one of them recognized by Jonquil was confirmation that they were who she thought they were.

"What happened," Jacinta asked. "Last I remember, Caro and I were talking about walking down after the lieutenant, and then . . ."

She went silent as Gallain shot her a look and made a cutting motion across his throat, then she gave a nod, her lips pursed closed.

"We were sitting around the fireplace." Ivan leaned forward. "Talking . . . nonsense. Like dream language, where nothing makes sense."

"It was a spell." Genevieve said. "Everything he does involves a spell."

"And we left . . ." Caro's words were soft, and she let them trail off. She put her head in her hands. "We were idiots."

"I think maybe we were idiots because we were under a spell." Jacinta's voice was soft, as if she suspected they were being listened to. "I can't remember much after we turned off the main road."

Ivan sucked in a breath. "Me, either."

Gallain knocked his head back against the wall again. "That's on me."

"That's on *him*." Caro glared at the door to the side of them, as if suspecting their abductor was right outside. "Not that I have any idea who *he* is."

"Nasty, is what he is." Ric's voice was rough, and he cleared his throat. "He'll be coming in soon with food and water."

Almost as if he had been waiting to be announced, the door opened on a screech of rusty hinges, and their tormentor walked in, pulling a small cart behind him.

Again, Viviane saw evidence that this was usual for him, to have a packed prison full of captives. He had organized things so that it was easy to feed them all at once, without having to make multiple trips.

"How long have you been doing this?" she asked as he stopped well short of the soldiers' reach.

He sucked in a quick, surprised breath at the question, staring at her. "Long enough," he said.

She had been careful to study him covertly over the few days he'd come in to feed them. He seemed too thin, and he looked haggard. His hair was a mix of brown and gray, and his clothing hung off his frame. He moved as if he was injured, and the thought gave her a searing sense of satisfaction.

His mouth was set in a hard, uncompromising line but the few times he'd spoken, his voice had a soft, melodious tone. His voice didn't match anything else about him.

He shifted his focus from her to the soldiers, and for the first time, his mouth quirked in a smile. His eyes twinkled, and he looked like he was thoroughly enjoying himself.

"Wondering where the other two you were talking about around your camp fire are?" he asked. "That sometimes happens. One or other gets lost in the forest. Especially if they're lagging behind."

"Where are they, then?" Gallain asked.

"Coming soon enough. I sent someone to bring them to me."

The soldiers leaned back, looking unhappy, but Viviane saw Gallain and Caro share a look, as if there was a chance things weren't going to go quite the way their abductor thought they would.

"What are you after?" Jacinta asked. "Why did you take the children?"

"They shone like a lighthouse beacon, and drew me in." He began sliding food through the grate as he spoke. "You and you," he pointed to Gallain and Caro, "you have a glimmer of it, but not enough to be of any real use. And you two have nothing." He flicked a hand at Ivan and Jacinta."

"Shone like a beacon?" Jacinta raised her eyebrows in question.

"With magic," he exclaimed. "Bright and clear. I'll need to separate them out, see who's generating most of it, but all of them have some. It created a kind of synergy out in the fields. Quite astonishing."

"And why do you steal children with magic?" Ivan asked.

"Not just children, although they are the most lucrative of my acquisitions." He closed the grate, then set the food and water for the soldiers on a tray on the floor and pushed it, sliding it toward them while still remaining a safe distance away. "I wouldn't have taken you four, even with the two who have a little magic, because I don't deal in the non-magical any more, but I overheard you say you were looking for the children, and I couldn't have you wandering around Warven, asking questions, no matter how idiotic they are in the town."

He seemed to expect a response, and when no one said anything, he gave another smile, and left.

Everyone must have thought he was still lurking outside the door, because no one said a word, and after a long wait, finally Viviane heard the cart rattling away.

"He doesn't deal in the non-magical *any more*." Jacinta's words were hushed. "Did he say that?"

"He called us acquisitions." Jon tipped his weight forward, so he was balanced in a crouch on his toes. "He plans to . . . sell us?"

"After he works out which of us has the most magic." Genevieve looked up to the window. "I don't have any. I don't know what he's talking about."

"My mother thinks the Cervantes do have magic." Viviane spoke carefully. "And let me guess, Gallain and Caro are Cervantes?"

The two soldiers looked at each other in surprise, and then over to her.

Her friends were staring at her, too.

"What are you talking about?" Ric asked.

"It's the way we move. There's a reason we were once put into camps by the old Kassian queen. My mother and General Ru of the Venyatu have both said it, lots of times." She didn't know if she should have told them, didn't even know if her mother and the general's guesses were right, but it felt like something she shouldn't keep to herself.

"I have thought there is something magical in the way your father moves," Ivan said, suddenly. "I've never seen someone so intuitive in a fight. But then I thought . . ." He cleared his throat and looked uncomfortable.

"You thought it might be his magical sword?" Viviane asked.

Caro snorted and turned to look at her friend. "You think the Commander's sword is magical?"

Ivan shrugged sheepishly. "It's a rumor."

"It's been a rumor since he came back with it from north Kassia to rejoin the Rising Wave," Gallain said. "But I once heard someone ask him, and he laughed and said it really is just a sword."

"My mother thinks there's a Cervantes magic. Something the Cervantes are born with. A magical connection between body and mind." Viviane had seen her father smile when her mother said things like that, then kiss the top of her head and whisper about getting a little help from his wife.

Her mother had stitched magic into her father's skin when he was wounded, to heal him. But that had been before Viviane was even born. Neither of her parents knew if it was still active, although most likely not. But her mother still protected her father with every piece of clothing she made him, every stitch of embroidery she put into everything he wore.

Her mother didn't go anywhere without needle and thread.

Vivi had neither right now, as she had been taken in her sleeping clothes and her abductor had taken their things. But stitch work was not her only weapon. Any kind of weaving, including braiding hair, could work. But as she'd decided when she'd first awoken, that was too dangerous to do when there was no plan. He said he could see their magic. Best to make none, then, until it really counted.

"Who was the man talking about? Saying he's having another two brought to him?" Jon asked.

Jacinta glanced toward the door, then spoke in a soft voice. "Lieutenant Theo Hallan, and Melodie."

"Theo?" Viviane's voice shook. "He's caught?"

"That one seems to think so," Ivan said, jerking his thumb at the door. "I'm not so sure."

Viviane heard the words, but she curled over her knees. She thought she remembered him being captured once before, the first night they'd been taken, but that had turned out to be wrong. She wouldn't think about him being captured again.

Because if he was, the hope that had bloomed inside her would be crushed.

CHAPTER 22

KANDRA GUS LOOKED QUITE NORMAL, if you couldn't see the net over his head and shoulders.

Theo kept looking at him in quick, suspicious glances, as if he couldn't quite believe his level of cooperation, but Melodie could see the net, and she never forgot they were using this man.

He would have used them. He would have delivered them to Marchant for money, and she held that thought firm in her head every time she felt guilt at his willing agreement to everything they said.

He had walked out of town with them, down the road to Nena's farm, and then Theo stopped, stepping close to her and bending his head.

"You stay back when he goes to the clearing, Melodie. You keep well back." He reached out and gripped her shoulder fiercely. "I'll be waiting for him, but I don't want you in his sights."

She could say that she'd agreed with him when they planned this, that she knew what she had to do, but he looked so worried, she simply inclined her head. "I will."

"It's not just because you're the only one who can see his traps," he said. "That's part of it, but you will not fall into his hands because I don't want him touching a hair on your head."

She found no words for that. He squeezed her shoulder, and then turned, vaulting the fence and getting past the web before leaping back into the road.

"Give me twenty minutes," he said, still looking unhappy. He hesitated. "I don't like splitting up."

"This is the best way," she reminded him, and he gave a curt nod and walked backward for a few steps before turning and jogging away.

Melodie watched him go, and when Gus started after him, she touched his arm and asked him to wait with her awhile and chat.

"How many people have you brought to Marchant over the years?" she asked. She might as well find out as much as she could.

Gus rocked back and forward on his heels. "I really don't know how many he's taken, but it's nothing to do with me." He seemed agitated. "I'm not getting involved in his slave trade."

Melodie felt as if someone had run a handful of snow down the back of her neck. "Slave trade?" She tried to keep her voice steady.

"He looks for travelers with lots of magic and he sells them to powerful people." Gus lifted his shoulders, then gave a shiver. "Gives me the creeps. I won't be having it. I told him I draw the line there."

"How did he take that?" Melodie asked.

Gus twisted his lips. "He didn't kick up as much of a fuss as I thought. I actually think it made him trust me more. Besides, it's hard to take people. Steal too many, and people start coming to look for them. So he only does it if they can do something really spectacular, and that isn't often, he tells me."

"But he has to take them first, to work out what they can do?" she asked. "What does he do with the ones that aren't any use to him?"

"That's the interesting thing. He sends them into the forest. Dumps them somewhere, he's never told me where, but a lot of them end up in Warven a day or two later, sort of confused and babbling. He's got a couple of the town guards in his pocket, and they spin stories of a strain of mushrooms which release spores that cause fever dreams."

"That's actually pretty clever," Melodie said. She tried to keep her tone upbeat. The clearing in the forest with the magic box had obviously served double-duty. He used it to entrap his victims, and, if they weren't of enough value to him, he used it to befuddle them into thinking it had all been a bad dream.

"Better than killing them," Gus said, lifting his hands. "That would get as messy as taking too many of them."

But he *had* taken too many. A lifetime of caution, and he'd suddenly grabbed four children all at once. Melodie wondered what was going on.

"And the people in the town don't raise an eyebrow at all these lost souls wandering in?" she asked.

"The people in this town are a little . . . off," Gus said. "I'd almost believe the spore story, if I didn't know Marchant made it up."

"You said you don't get involved in taking people, but you were going to grab Theo with the net, and I'm assuming use Nena to help take me along, too." Melodie thought it was almost time to go. Theo would be in place by now.

"He wasn't going to take you. He was going to question you and put you in the forest afterward, he said. I wouldn't have done it, otherwise."

"I see. That's all right, then."

Gus smiled at her happily.

"Well, let's get going. Why don't you lead the way?" she said.

He moved down the road obediently, and she watched carefully as he walked through the web.

It melted as he touched it, and she couldn't see any other reaction. She was very interested to learn how it worked.

Just to be sure there wasn't more to it, that it didn't pacify or lull its victims, she climbed the fence, walked around the wooden pole, and then climbed back over. She had to hurry to catch up to Gus, who forged ahead.

She let him go at his own pace. Marchant would know how long it usually took him to reach the meeting spot after he walked through the web, and she didn't want to interfere with that. Much.

"Wait," she called, just as he reached the gap in the hedge that led to the meeting place.

He stopped, looking at her expectantly.

"You can tell Marchant you weren't able to capture me and the lieutenant, because we'd already left early this morning."

She was wearing her riding gloves and she hovered nearby, ready to pull the net off Gus just before they reached the clearing.

She didn't know how quickly he'd come back to himself, and whether he'd understand what had happened to him, but she decided it was worth the risk.

If Marchant saw him wearing the net, he would know nothing Gus said was true.

"I wasn't?" he asked. "Is that right?"

"It's to stop you getting in trouble with him," she reminded him. "You failed because the confusion isn't so strong in the town anymore."

"Oh, yes." He said it slowly. "The inn was full, too. It was clear they were more aware. You were more aware."

She nodded, and he nodded back.

"Thank you. Yes, that is a good story to tell." He turned down the narrow path and as he did, she lifted the net off him, holding it away from her body.

She let him walk on, and she used her other hand to scrunch the net up into a tiny ball, then pulled the glove on her hand off, turning it inside out and wrapping the net up in it. She slid it into her coat pocket, and kept her other glove on.

She could almost hear the shouting of her father from beyond the grave for putting herself so close to someone who trafficked in people just like her.

Then she shut the door on the voice and slid into the woods, keeping off the path, moving slowly to make as little sound as possible.

She heard voices from up ahead, and crept closer, but there were too many chances to be seen, so she got down on hands and knees and crawled forward until she could hear the conversation.

"What do you mean, they aren't confused anymore?" Marchant's voice was deep and smooth. It was a shock to hear him.

"They aren't like they usually are. Vague, you know? Forgetful."

"You noticed that?" Marchant asked.

"It was obvious. But whatever was making them so befuddled seems to have gone." Gus sounded cheerful.

"And those two who came in late last night were gone in the morning?"

"Left early, the innkeeper said. Back to Illoa."

Marchant swore softly. "All right. Go stay at Nena's for two days, then go back to the inn. If they went to fetch reinforcements, they'll take at least a day to get to Illoa, a day to get back, but most likely more."

"Go back to the inn to do what?" Gus asked.

"To see how many they come back with. What their plans are. Get one of them alone and use the net to ask them questions." Marchant sounded annoyed to have to spell it out.

"I can do that. Nena won't like me staying there, she's not so befuddled anymore, either. But she's done too much now to say no." Gus shuffled, she could hear his clothes rustling.

"I'd forgotten she was affected, too." Marchant spoke softly. "I'm going to have to go check—." He stopped himself short. "I'll see you in three days. Same time. Whether the soldiers are back from Illoa or not, meet me here to pass on what you've learned."

"Right'o." Gus turned and walked away, whistling under his breath, as if he didn't have a care in the world.

She didn't hear any movement, as if Marchant were standing watching after him, either deep in thought or looking for any sign he was followed.

Finally she heard a sigh, the rustle of boots through leaves, and then silence.

She held.

Theo would have a good view of Marchant, that's why he went ahead to hide. Theo would let her know when it was safe.

But he never called out.

She wished now that her ring could fit on her finger under her glove, but she'd had to take it off. It would be good to have warning if danger lurked.

She lay absolutely still, worry building in her, and then someone ran straight for her.

Theo wouldn't do that, so she reached in her pocket and pulled out her glove, scrambled to her feet just in time to catch glimpses of a thin man with dark face coverings dodging through the thick bush to get to her.

She pulled out the net from inside the other glove as he burst into view.

He stopped, almost comical in the way he had to windmill his arms to keep his balance. His eyes were fixed on the net.

"That's the glow I saw." He flicked his gaze to her, then frowned. "Or you're glowing, as well as the net." He shook his head, as if unsure. "What's that in your bag?"

"I'll tell you all about it," she said, flicking the net toward him, but he gave a sharp cry at the sight of it billowing out, and dove away.

She heard him scramble through the brush and then the sound of his footsteps running through dead leaves until they faded away.

She fought her way through branches and scratchy bushes to the path, then ran to the clearing.

"Theo?"

Had Marchant found him? Enspelled him before he spoke with Gus?

That made no sense, because he seemed to have believed Gus's story.

Unless he thought Theo had followed the town guard who'd

come to report to Marchant about their arrival last night. Gus had said he'd passed the man on his way to his own meeting.

But if Marchant had seen Theo, he'd know he was the same person he'd enspelled before. She shook her head. There were too many what-ifs.

She studied the open space, saw the bell was still on the log, glowing softly with its magic.

She stepped beyond it, found where Marchant must stand and watch the people coming to seek an audience with him, then turned slowly, looking for where Theo might have chosen to hide.

She walked carefully around the outside of the clearing, stepping around trees and bushes, keeping an ear out in case Marchant came back with some kind of weapon—which he surely would.

She had weapons of her own, though. She had the net, the small handful of confusion dust she'd rescued from the box in the forest, and the paint set. Those weren't to be discounted.

She wondered if he had actually seen magic in her, or whether it was the paint set, with its almost blinding glow, leaking out of her bag. Either way, he hadn't been sure, and that was to her advantage.

She had never thought of herself as actually being magical. She could see it, not make it.

She wasn't under any illusion about the value of that, though. And neither would Marchant be. A shiver ran down her back at the thought of what he would do with her if he ever understood her abilities.

A faint glimmer of light seemed to come from beneath the leaf-covered ground up ahead, and she slowed, skirting around the area, carefully extending a stick she found and poking at the forest floor. There was a place where it looked as if the ground had fallen away into a dark hole, but when she got closer, she saw it was a net, stretched over a pit, and it had pulled down on one side. The ropes were thick and made of hemp, rather than the gossamer silk of the one in her glove.

She hooked the stick under it, and heaved upward, dislodging leaves, but unable to move it up very much.

She almost tripped over the first stake, and she walked around the hole, working them free, and then pulled, so one whole side of the net fell into the hole.

She peered in and found Theo looking up at her. His hair and shoulders were covered in leaves, his hands and face dirt-streaked. "Melodie."

She lifted a finger to her lips and he fell silent. Then she stepped to the edge and studied the trap.

It wasn't that deep. On the face of it, Theo could climb out, so something was obviously stopping him.

She pulled the net completely clear of the hole and set it to one side. The moment it was completely away from the trap, she heard Theo's labored breathing.

It had been dampening the sound from the hole. She gave it another look, saw the faint glimmer of light in the weave.

She shook her head. Had she ever encountered so many spell-worked objects in one place?

She stepped back to the edge of the hole and then crouched down, studying it.

Theo stood in a warrior stance, eyes narrowed, sword drawn.

After a moment, she rose and began to walk slowly around the hole, looking for the reason he couldn't escape.

Theo moved with her, keeping her directly above him as she moved, and she finally noticed it. A thin line hooked into his coat, tethered to the ground.

Even as she saw it, Theo tried to climb up again, hands scrabbling in the dark, loose soil.

The line pulled him back.

She checked she still had her knife on her belt, then she jumped down into the hole.

The look of horror on Theo's face made her suddenly doubt herself, as if there was another danger she hadn't noticed.

"What the fuck, Mel?" He breathed the words in her ear as he pulled her close. She smelled sweat, and earth, and something so deliciously Theo, it sent a shiver through her. "You're not supposed to throw yourself into the trap with me."

"I'm cutting you free." She pulled back, knife in hand, and crouched beside him. Then, having an idea, she pulled her glove tight and carefully worked the hook out of his jacket without even having to cut.

She studied it, but couldn't see how it had hooked into Theo's coat. And they didn't have time for her to work it out.

She walked back to where it was tethered, and hooked the end into the iron loop that was buried in the ground.

"We should destroy it, but I don't think we have time for that right now."

He stood beside her, shook his head. "I can't even see it. I don't even know what it is."

She straightened. "That's why I'm here. We need to go," she said, and he nodded, turned, and ran up the side of the hole and was up on the lip, looking down at her, in a moment.

He crouched, hand down, and she grabbed it, let herself be hauled up.

"Does Marchant know you fell into this?" she asked him, as soon as they were both away from the edge.

"I don't know. I didn't see him." Theo looked furious with himself. "I fell in before he even arrived, I think."

"Then let's put the net back. I don't think he knew you were here. Maybe it's a trap that doesn't warn him. Maybe he has to check it periodically. But I frightened him with the compliance net, so he ran away." She moved to the net and Theo helped her stake it back in the ground over the hole.

Most of the leaves that had disguised the net had fallen into the pit when she'd pulled it free, but even as they finished stretching it across, more fell from above.

"So, where did Marchant go?" Theo asked her. His sword was back in his hand.

"He ran up the hill through the forest, but who knows if he kept going in that direction. I threatened him with the net and he bolted."

"He would not want to have that net on him," Theo said softly. "He would lose all control."

"Also." Melodie hesitated, then fluttered her hands in distress. "Gus told me . . ."

Theo had moved closer to her, his gaze worried. "What is it?"

"He said . . ." She drew in a breath. "He said that Marchant has run a slave trade for years. I can only believe the children are his latest victims."

Theo went very still, and she could see him trying to bank his rage. "How has he managed to keep from drawing attention to himself all these years?"

"Maybe because he sells to powerful people." She didn't think any but the truly wealthy could afford to buy a magical person.

She had lived with the fear of it happening to her, but sometimes she wondered if the fear was overblown. Now she knew better.

"Well, he's come to my attention, now," Theo said. "And I'm going to make him regret it."

CHAPTER 23

THE DOOR BURST OPEN, and Marchant—because the soldiers had told them that was his name—stepped in, sides heaving, hand gripping his hip.

He caught Viviane's eye, grimaced in pain, and did a quick scan of the room, visibly counting heads. Then he stepped back and she heard the door lock behind him.

She could hear him running down the gravel path.

He hadn't spoken a single word.

"Theo," Gallain murmured. "Theo got him thinking his captives might be gone."

"Or Melodie," Caro said.

"Maybe," Ivan agreed, nodding. "So how do we get ready to run?"

"We've been mulling that for days," Jon said. "We're out of ideas."

"What about the tray?" Caro said. "It looks like it's metal."

The soldiers had eaten their food and the tray was empty except for the water jug.

"Possible," Ivan agreed, pulling it closer. He set the jug aside and stood, holding the tray horizontally.

He lifted his massive arms, aimed at the metal disc that held the chain to the wall, angled it, and smashed it down.

The tray buckled.

Ivan swore, his face a little red, and he bent the tray inward with his bare hands.

"Marchant's had practice," Viviane said, so he didn't feel bad. "I think he's been holding people in here for a very long time."

"He's got every possible means of escape covered. Maybe a few managed to get out in the beginning, and he learned all the weak points." Jacinta flopped back against the wall.

"You think Theo bested him, somehow?" Viviane asked, because she wanted to hold onto the little flare of hope burning inside her.

"He clearly doesn't have Theo, and he thought we might have been rescued, which is why he came in here all wild-eyed." Gallain shrugged. "That's got to be good for us."

Yes, that had to be good for them. And Theo had never, ever let her down.

Illoa was a blur.

Captain Draper had been expecting them. Had supplies waiting, and fresh mounts.

Ava knew Luc was as impressed as she was. Captain Draper would be moving up in the ranks, without a doubt.

"Do you still want me to watch the goat?" Draper asked, leaning in to talk softly to Luc, although Ava was close enough to hear her.

"The goat?" Ava asked.

They were saddling horses, a little way from the others, so that Luc could have a final, private word with Draper.

"The goat I'm watching in the square," Draper said. "Theo was turned into a goat the first night he chased after the children. He suggested I put a goat in the square, just in case the spell worker found the trader, learned what he'd done with it, and came back for it. Him." She shook her head in confusion. "He didn't understand why the trader had tied him to the bridge, but he thought it was worth keeping watch, just on the off-chance the abductor came back to look for it . . . him."

"That is a very good plan." Luc clasped her shoulder. "You have people watching?"

Draper nodded. "Night and day. Two or three at a time. And I switch them often, so it's not so obvious."

"If we miss the abductor, or something goes wrong, it's a good failsafe." Ava nodded. "It's your top priority."

Draper lifted a fist and bumped it against her chest.

"You've done very well, Captain." Luc turned to hoist Ava up into her saddle. "Keep your ear to the ground. If you hear anything strange, see anyone trying to cross into Kassia and Cervantes that makes you twitchy, you have full permission to detain."

"Do the Grimwaldians know what's happening?" Draper asked.

"Not yet. Let's clear it up first and then we'll tell them." He swung into his own saddle, and they were off, galloping over the bridge into Grimwalt.

Ava thought of the friends she had in Taunen, Grimwalt's capital. Some were on the council there. There would be no diplomatic issues from them about her unannounced entry into her former homeland when they knew what had happened.

Someone in Grimwalt, someone with some oversight, should have known about a spell worker this strong. And how had he dared take four children—*four*—from the Cervantes plains, and thought there would be no repercussions?

"What are you thinking?" Luc asked as they made it through the town and out to the open road to Taunen.

She tried to wind back her rage so she could answer him. "I managed to get free of my captors just before I reached Illoa, all those years ago." Ava remembered the pure relief of escape, even though she had been so weak from the rope that had been used on her, she had struggled to walk any distance without needing a rest. "Whatever's happened to Viviane, she hasn't been able to escape."

And that terrified her. Her daughter had the skills she had never had at that age. Unlike her own mother, Ava had made sure Vivi knew what her magic could do and how to use it.

It was only a little sad to her that her son, at ten years old, showed no sign of having the same magical talent.

"It doesn't mean she's injured. It just means she hasn't found a way out yet." Luc moved his horse closer to her.

Ava forced herself to nod. "This is what happened to my mother. Twice. To me. Twice." She blinked back the moisture dimming her eyesight.

"Hey, now." Luc reached over and gently tugged at her hair. It had been so short when they'd first met, shorn by her cousin so she couldn't use it to embroider with. "Theo is right behind her."

She nodded again. "Did you ask Draper who the spell worker was who went with him?"

Luc swore softly. "I'd forgotten about her. No, I didn't."

"It doesn't matter. Nothing matters but getting Vivi back." She drew herself up. "Getting them all back."

She wanted them all safe at home, along with Bastien, her son, who was being looked after by a whole unit of guards right now in Ta-lin. She wanted her family together.

"We will." Luc touched the hilt of his sword in an unconscious movement. "We will."

CHAPTER 24

THEY WENT NORTH WEST, following Marchant.

Theo made sure Melodie was happy there were no traps with every turn they took in the clearly marked path.

He still couldn't believe she had found him in that pit. He had felt entombed in the shallow hole, and he knew magic must have been at work. He had drunk in the sight of her as he brushed leaves out of his hair and eyes, relieved and elated beyond words.

He'd felt like an idiot. He had been so focused on checking Marchant's hidey hole's line of sight in relation to where he planned to hunker down, he hadn't watched his feet.

But Marchant hadn't found him, and Melodie had frightened the spell caster off.

Theo didn't like it that he knew she even existed.

"You're brooding." Melodie shot him a slightly amused look.

He couldn't help the quick uptick of his lips. "I don't brood. I glower."

"Ah. Apologies." She smiled.

"How did Marchant find you?" he asked.

"He said he saw the glow of the net, but he couldn't have. I only took it out when I heard him running toward me."

"What do you think it was, then?" Theo kept his voice low, but they would need to understand this before they confronted him again.

"I think it was the paint box. It almost blinded me when I first saw it, and he said he saw a glow."

Theo had forgotten about the paint box. "You brought it?"

She shrugged. "No use to us back in the inn. And it could be useful."

But was also a beacon for Marchant.

"Let's wrap it up." Theo shrugged off his pack, opened it up, and lifted out a spare shirt Captain Draper had given him.

Melodie shook her head. "That won't do."

She crouched down, opened her own pack, and took out the paint box. She set it on the ground, and then began to pull out everything inside her pack.

"Why won't the shirt do?" Theo asked.

She looked up at him. "It's spelled itself. The glow is barely there, but it isn't nothing."

"What?" He had to force himself to keep his voice down. "Spelled, how?"

"With protection." She held his gaze briefly, then looked back down at the pile she'd made on the ground. "Almost all the Kassia and Cervantes soldiers wear those shirts. If I see one walking around Illoa without one, then my guess is the protection shirt is in the wash."

"We all wear shirts that are spelled to protect us." He said it quietly, and a picture came to mind of the queen sitting in the afternoon sun, needle and thread in hand, with a pile of shirts beside her.

He had always thought it was an endearing tradition, that every soldier in the army received a shirt hand-stitched by their queen when they were accepted into the corps.

She had been protecting them all. The thought was staggering.

And then he remembered little Viviane, sitting by her mother's side, learning how to do it, and a wave of fear so icy-cold swept over him, he gasped.

"What is it?" Melodie had frozen in place, her expression fearful.

"I . . ." He swallowed. "I think the princess is why Marchant was attracted to the students. I think . . ." He shook himself. "We have to move fast. He knows we're here now, he knows we're close. If he's going to move the children, sell them or whatever he does with his prisoners, he'll be doing it even faster now."

"Viviane is responsible for the shirts?" Melodie said, shaking her head. "I thought she was only thirteen years old."

"Not her." He didn't want to say anymore.

Melodie slid a book out of a leather pouch, worked the paint box into it, although the fit was tight, and drew the drawstring closed. She frowned at the book, then shoved it right at the bottom of the pack, put the pouch on top and then the rest of her things.

She stood, then walked around it, studying it, and finally satisfied, slung it back over her shoulder.

"Her mother?" she said, as if the break in the conversation hadn't occurred. "The queen?"

Theo lifted his shoulders, but it was the obvious conclusion.

"I knew someone, long ago, who had that magic. She saved my life." She glanced at him. "No one will ever hear anything from me about this."

Theo gave a nod, shoved the precious shirt right to the bottom of his own pack and then secured the top so it was completely closed. "We have to go."

"It can't be far," Melodie said, as they started abreast on the path again. "We've been walking for at least fifteen minutes."

She was right. Just ahead, Theo caught a glimpse of roofs, and put out a hand to stop Melodie.

She looked carefully around them, searching for traps, and then they stepped off the path into the forest.

He made sure they moved together, and when the way got harder, he let Melodie go in front.

Eventually they worked their way to the outer edge of the wood that encircled Marchant's compound, which was set on a little plateau on the side of the hill.

Theo crouched down against a thick tree trunk and Melodie sat down and leaned back against it, facing down the hill, the way they'd come. She pulled out her water flask and drank, then offered it to him.

Theo took a few sips, his gaze on the buildings rising up in front of him.

There were four.

A small cottage, which looked unkempt on the outside, with overgrown flowerbeds below the windows and paint peeling off shutters.

There was a stable, and he could smell horses on the light breeze, and then two other buildings.

One was set a little away from the other three, and whatever it was for, it looked the best maintained.

He was about to ask Melodie to take a look at the area around the buildings for any signs of spell work, when Marchant stepped out of the forest that curved around to the left of where Theo had hunkered down. It looked like he'd come down the hill.

Melodie must have been watching him, because she rose up into a crouch at his reaction and moved right next to him so she could also see Marchant as he walked along the path to the cluster of three buildings.

He moved slowly, stopping twice to catch his breath, and his hand went to his side.

Theo felt a surge of satisfaction. He hadn't known exactly where he had stabbed Marchant, but he was sure now it was in the side.

Marchant stopped again, but this time it was to move off the path, then stepped back onto it a few steps later, and Theo committed the place he'd avoided to memory.

There would be a nasty trap there, of that he was sure.

He guessed Marchant would go to the cottage, but instead he

stepped onto a gravel path that led to the building next to the stables, unlocked it, and stepped inside.

He wondered whether it might be where Marchant was keeping his prisoners, and then Marchant appeared again, pushing someone in front of him.

Viviane. Her dark hair was pulled into a long braid down her back.

Marchant prodded her all the way to the fourth building, and then disappeared inside with her.

The relief Theo felt was immense. She was alive, and looked uninjured. And he knew where she was.

Everything else could be fixed.

While the coast was clear, he rose up and stepped out of the tree line. Melodie came to stand beside him.

"He came out of the forest over there." Theo pointed.

"I wondered where he was?" she said. "Checking over the hill on the confusion spell, maybe? Gus told him it wasn't working anymore."

"Maybe." It would explain why he had been moving with such difficulty. It had to be a mile at least, up and down hill from here to the clearing in the forest.

"That's his house, the stables, his prison," Melodie murmured, looking at the three buildings grouped together. "So what's the purpose of the one he's taken Viviane to? His workshop?"

His workshop? That sounded all too possible. And frightening.

Because a man like that worked on nothing good.

CHAPTER 25

MARCHANT PRODDED her down a path toward a wooden building set away from the others and Viviane kept her body upright and moved faster so he wouldn't touch her as often.

She had known this was coming.

He'd already told them he would have to work out where most of their magic was coming from, and she'd guessed that wasn't going to happen in the prison cells.

He said he could see magic in people, but obviously not easily, or he would know just by looking at them.

But she'd been thinking of a way to fool him, and after he'd burst in, checking to see they were still in the cells, and then disappeared again, she'd begun to braid her hair.

Her actions had gone virtually unnoticed by the others as they spoke quietly about ways to escape.

She'd woven a spell into the braid that would hopefully hide her magic. Her mother had taught her how to braid protection into her hair before, but she had never tried to make her magic invisible. She had never considered anyone could see the magic in her.

She had learned from her mother how to weave or stitch invisibility into cloth. If she could make herself invisible, maybe she could do the same to her magic.

When she was done, she'd offered to braid Genevieve's hair, and had done the same to her.

There was no braiding the boys' hair. They wore their hair short, like her father.

He had set the trend amongst his soldiers, although he made no rules about how they should wear it.

Because of their close alliance with the Venyatux, who wore their hair in long, complex braids, man or woman, any style went in the Kassia and Cervantes military. But most, especially the new recruits, modeled their look on her father, who wore his hair short, so no one could get a handhold on it.

It was a pity, but there was nothing she could do and the boys were not as magical as she was. Or, she didn't think so.

Even though she was being taken somewhere on her own, she enjoyed stretching her legs after days of being chained to a wall, but the gravel was rough on her bare feet, and she winced as Marchant gave her another little shove to hurry her along.

"In," he said when they reached the door, and then gave her a little push over the threshold.

She stepped in and he locked the door behind them.

They were instantly plunged into darkness and she stopped dead.

Just before he'd closed them in, she'd caught a glimpse of a table, what she thought might be more chains on the wall, and some other equipment she hadn't the time to identify.

She heard the scrape of a match, and light bloomed behind her.

The chains were very real. And it made her chest tighten so much, she could barely breathe.

Marchant skirted around her, still holding the chain he'd set around her wrists when he'd unlocked her from the shackles she shared with Gen, and when she saw he was not carrying a light, she realized he must have lit a small sconce on the wall by the door.

She stood still, trying to make out everything she could through the gloom, but the chain stretched out to its full length and he jerked her forward.

Her standing still jerked him a little, as well, and it must have hurt him, or caused him pain where he was injured.

He turned on her, face feral with rage. "Move."

She moved, walking toward him, still gauging her surroundings, and when she got within reach of him, he slapped her. Hard.

She stopped again, astonished. Her cheek throbbed at the hit, and she knew her mouth had fallen open.

"You will listen, or you will be punished, understood?"

She gave a nod, fighting back the tears that stung her eyes.

He stared at her. "I had a feeling you were the main contributor to the glow that night I found you, but your individual light is weak, now I can see you again in the darkness. What can you do?"

"I can fight," she said, trying to keep the relief that her braid spell had worked from her voice. "All Cervantes can."

He started to shake his head, and then went still. "I have seen a glow from the Kassia and Cervantes soldiers, some stronger than others, but I always put that down to the shirts."

The shirts.

Viviane tried not to look sick. Her mother's shirts had been out in the world for more than fifteen years. Of course this creature had come across people wearing them.

"The shirts are a special gift for entering the army," she said. "I hope to earn one, one day."

"But some of the soldiers are Kassian, aren't they? And others are Cervantes." Marchant began to circle her, muttering to himself. "Maybe the stronger ones are just Cervantes in the shirt. A natural magical talent for fighting, added to the shirt's protective magic. That's why some glow brighter." Suddenly he stopped, as if remembering something. "Your cloak."

She had almost forgotten about her cloak. "Yes?"

"It was full of spell work. Protection of every kind."

"My aunt gave me that coat for my birthday," she said.

"And who is your aunt?" He looked disbelieving.

"She is Massi of North Grimwalt. The wife of Duncan, Keeper of the North." She hoped this did not come back in a bad way to Aunt Massi. She knew her favorite of her parents' friends would hug her and tell her, whoever was causing her to make up stories to protect herself should be worried nothing bad came back on *them*. And then she would notch an arrow in her bow.

"Massi of the North." He stopped cold, staring at her in astonishment.

"My father and her are family," Vivi said, and although they really weren't blood siblings, they had forged a bond in the Chosen camps that made them brother and sister in all but blood. And they would probably say enough of their blood had spilled and mingled to make that part true, too.

"I wonder where she got it," he said, walking over to a table covered by a tarpaulin. He drew it back, stepping away a little as if seeing something she could not.

Finally, in the weak light, she recognized that it was a pile made up of their clothing, that he'd stolen from them.

He stepped back to the table, sorted through the pile, and lifted up her cloak. "It's a work of art."

"I see you're a thief," she said. She couldn't help it.

He stopped, turned and looked at her speculatively. "I am. A very good one. Of people and magical things." He touched the shirt he was wearing beneath his coat. "I'm wearing a Kassia and Cervantes' soldier's shirt right now. I take them whenever I can." He fingered the collar. "Not that it helped me the other day."

He had been injured and the shirt hadn't protected him.

"Spell work only lasts so long," she said. "And those shirts are for soldiers in the army. Not the thieves who take them."

He studied her for a beat. "Maybe. Spell work is tricky like that. That's why I prefer to deal in people, not things. The magic inside them lasts for their lifetime."

Having it said so starkly, knowing how well-oiled his system of feeding and confining his prisoners was, brought it home to her that this man had taken a lot of people in his time.

It was a horrifying thought.

Even in the dim light her face must have shown that horror, because he stared at her, watching her with a passive, almost curious expression.

"You find me revolting." He said it matter-of-factly.

She didn't even bother to answer.

He suddenly gripped her coat tightly to him, hugging it close. "At least this cloak makes the whole exercise not a complete loss. I will have to find some way to dump you and those soldiers, now that my usual method has been destroyed."

Whatever had been destroyed she guessed was down to Uncle Theo. Had to be.

Vivi kept her face still, but she was doing a little dance inside.

"Of course, unless most of the glow I saw was from the cloak, one of your little friends might still be magical enough to be interesting to me. Let's go." He walked past her and opened the door, and she followed dutifully behind. Her cheek still throbbed from earlier.

Marchant gave a yank of the chain, and she stumbled a little to catch up, keeping her mouth closed in a thin, tight line.

She wanted her mother and her father. She wanted this to end.

If Theo had come after them, then logically Uncle Rafe had gone for help. Her parents would be racing to the rescue, with a full cohort in tow.

She knew that. She knew everything that could be done to find them was being done.

She just wanted it to be done now.

CHAPTER 26

THE PRINCESS WORE a spell in her hair. Melodie said nothing about it until Marchant disappeared with her into what she suspected were the holding cells.

She had seen a braiding spell like that before. She had had one woven into her own hair, although hers was for protection. This one was for something else. A dampening spell. Perhaps to hide the princess's magic.

She rocked back on her heels.

She had been thinking Marchant was like her. That he could see spell work. But when they'd come face to face earlier, he hadn't known whether the glow he'd seen from her was her own personal magic, or the compliance net. And also, perhaps, the paint set.

She wouldn't have made that same mistake.

"I see spells," she said.

Theo looked at her, frowning.

"I can see the glow of spell work, like a layer of light over whatever has been spelled." She paused. "I think Marchant can see magic. He sees it the same way I see spells, but he can't know if someone's magic is because they are using a spell-worked item, or because they themselves are magical."

"But because you only see spell work, you can't see magic inside someone. Can't see if they themselves are magical?" Theo spoke slowly.

"Exactly. I think the princess figured that out, or Marchant straight out told her. She wove a spell into her hair to make her magic seem much less than it is, is my guess, because I saw a dampening spell clearly as he took her back to the cells."

"You saw a spell in her hair?" Theo's eyes narrowed. "I just saw that she had clearly been hit in the face." He paused. "But the spell would make her hair shine with magic, wouldn't it?"

"It should have, because it was braided in, but the very nature of the spell itself was to hide magic. It might have been a gamble on Viviane's part on whether he'd see the magic, or whether the spell's function would work on his magical sight, but she had nothing to lose. And it looks like it might have worked." She remembered gentle fingers braiding her own hair when she was little, on the road trip she had never forgotten, of her lifting her plait to see the protection against knives and other weapons clearly.

"That was definitely the princess?" she asked. Because the princess was the right age to be a daughter of the woman who'd saved her all those years ago, but that would make her . . .

"I've known her since she was born," Theo said. "That is Viviane Franck."

"And her mother is Queen Ava of Kassia and Cervantes?"

He nodded.

It was a long time ago, but she had always thought the woman who was clearly being held against her will by one of the travelers in their caravan, and who saved Melodie before she escaped, was called Sue. And she hadn't been a queen. She had been from Grimwalt. She had apparently offered her father a place to stay in Grimwalt when they crossed the border, and every now and then, when times had gotten hard, her father would wonder out loud if he shouldn't have taken her up on her offer.

"Why do you ask?" Theo had turned away from her, looking over at the building Marchant used as a prison.

"I knew someone when I was very young who could braid spells into hair, but it's obviously possible more than one spell worker can do it."

"He's bringing out Genevieve." Theo's voice got lower.

Melodie watched Marchant pull a reluctant Genevieve along the gravel path. "She's got the same dampening spell in her hair."

Theo glanced at her. "That's good, right? Marchant will think they're both too weak magically to be interesting."

Melodie nodded in agreement.

They watched Genevieve come out as quickly as Viviane had, and then the boys were marched across one by one. The fourth boy looked like he was in pain as he walked, and Marchant seemed rougher on him.

"Ric hurt him," Theo murmured. "Even before I did. I'd forgotten about it, but one of the sticks at the camp had blood on it. I think Ric stabbed him with it. Marchant's done something to him in retaliation."

"He doesn't like being hurt, and he's almost paranoid about being overpowered or having the tables turned on him." Melodie watched Marchant shove the boy into the workshop. "He ran in a panic when he saw the compliance net."

"A true coward." As Theo spoke, Marchant emerged again, and Ric, limping behind him, looked slightly gray, as if he had been further harmed in the workshop.

Melodie felt a surge of rage at the man. These were children, and he was a monster.

After he returned Ric, Marchant shuffled at an even slower pace to his house, and disappeared inside.

"Let's go." Theo stood. "I want to find out if the rest of the team are in there with the children."

They ran across the grass, jumping over the path as soon as they could so that the prison and stables would block any view of them from the house. The trap Marchant had set on the path glowed faintly in the afternoon light, and Melodie could see it was overlayed over a handful of stones that had been sprinkled through the gravel.

She didn't have time to see what it did.

They reached the prison, but the only window was near the entrance, which would expose them to the view of anyone leaving the house.

The window was closed.

"I need a rock." Theo looked at the gravel path, but the stones were too small to break a window.

"I'll draw one. And some twine and a pencil, so we can communicate."

He had completely forgotten about the paint set, she realized. He blinked.

"And some rope, so we can pull the stone back up," he said. "They might not be able to throw it back. They could be in chains."

She shook her head. "It won't last long enough."

He swore. "I forgot how quickly it disappears."

She moved to the far corner of the back wall, so Marchant wouldn't see the glow of the paint set while she used it.

Theo stood guard as she drew the rock, the pencil, the twine. As soon as the pencil appeared, she handed it to Theo, along with a corner she'd torn from the sheet of paper.

He wrote a few words, wound the twine around the rock, the pencil and the paper, and ran around to the front.

Melodie followed him, peering around the corner to keep watch on the house.

Theo threw the rock at the window overarm, and it broke with a loud crack.

Theo ran back to her, crouching just around the corner.

"It sounded loud," she said. She watched the door of the house, but it stayed closed.

With luck, Marchant was sleeping somewhere, or tending his wounds. Maybe he hadn't heard the noise.

"He is so weak, and yet, I can't risk taking him on with the magical tricks he seems to have up his sleeves." Theo's voice was infused with frustration. "They are right here. Right behind this wall." He hit it lightly with his fist.

"We should check out his house," Melodie said. "If we can take him unawares, using the net or the confusion dust I still have in my pocket, we could contain him."

"I'd prefer to have the children safe before then," Theo said. "But if that's the only way, so be it."

CHAPTER 27

A ROCK CAME through the window.

It cracked the glass so loudly, Viviane jumped.

Her focus had been on Ric, who was slumped against the wall, looking as gray as he had the first day he'd woken up, and the rock had been a shock of sound—completely unexpected.

It hit one of the bars of their prison cell and spun back to the wall, and Ivan reached out and plucked it from the air.

He ripped a piece of paper off it, read it, and passed the scrap to Gallain.

"Theo." Gallain grinned.

Ivan snatched the paper back and began to write on it with a pencil that she saw now had been tied to the rock, and then he swore as it disappeared in his hand.

"Melodie," Caro breathed. "She painted it."

"The paper's real," Jacinta said, and Viviane saw it was the only thing that was still visible. Even the rock had disappeared.

"Can you reach the door?" Caro asked Gallain, who was closest to it. "Slip the paper under it?"

"Maybe." He glanced at Ivan and they both got to their feet, shuffling as close to the door as they could. Eventually they lay down, and Gallain stretched out an arm. The paper fit under the door, and it was jerked out of his fingers.

"Gallain?"

Vivi heard Theo's voice coming in a whisper from under the gap in door, and for the first time allowed herself to believe he was really there.

"Lieutenant. We're in here with the children."

"All four of you?"

She saw Gallain wince at the question, and realized he must feel foolish that they had all been so easily taken. "Yes."

"I'm glad you're safe. What's the layout in there?" Theo asked.

"We're chained to the wall under the window. The children are in a room with a wall of bars enclosing them, directly opposite us."

"We'll see if we can break open the door. Melodie will draw a crowbar."

Viviane tried to understand what he meant, and there was sudden silence, and she guessed he had slipped away.

Having gone outside earlier, she knew the building that was most likely Marchant's house faced the door, so every moment he crouched beside it opened him up to discovery.

"Who's Melodie?" Genevieve asked. "And what does he mean, 'draw a crowbar'?"

The four soldiers said nothing in response, and Viviane guessed they were probably under orders not to talk about Melodie's gifts.

The rock had disappeared, the pencil had done the same. Maybe this Melodie could draw things into being for a short time.

A moment later, there was a scratching sound, and then a crack of wood as Theo levered a crowbar against the door.

After only a few minutes, the noise stopped and she guessed the crowbar had disappeared, but almost immediately, he started again. Maybe Melodie was making more as he worked, so he would have a never-ending supply of them.

"So glad we brought her along," Ivan murmured. "That was a very good idea."

The others said nothing, but Viviane could see their full focus was on the door, and all of them were standing now, tense and ready for whatever was to come.

She rose herself, her gaze flicking to Jon, who nodded, and crouched beside Ric.

"Tell us what he did to you," he murmured. "We need to know."

"Run without me," Ric said. He was still sitting against the wall, eyes closed, and there was something wrong with the way he was breathing.

"Not going to happen," Jon said.

"Ric, you insult us," Vivi said softly. "We would never leave you. Never."

He opened his eyelids a little, so she just caught a glimpse of the bright blue of his eyes. "You must."

"Never," she said again. "I'd rather stay behind."

"He did something to me. I don't know what, but it hurts to move." Ric finally opened his eyes fully. "And just now, in that torture chamber, he hit me with a stick. I don't think it was a normal stick. There was some spell on it."

"Where?" she asked.

He touched his ribs. "It hurts to breathe."

She wished she had needle and thread. She wished his hair was longer. But wishing would accomplish nothing right now.

She would never sleep without a needle and thread wound into her clothing ever again.

"Gallain and I will carry you," Ivan said, his tone matter-of-fact, as if it were a foregone conclusion.

Ric looked like he wanted to argue, and Vivi pointed to him, then put a finger to her lips.

She saw his own lips quirk a little at her silent command to keep his mouth shut and accept he was going to be helped.

It was the first smile they'd gotten out of him since they'd been taken, and the sight of it lightened her heart.

And then her heart soared as the door gave a final crack and Theo shoved his shoulder into the gap and pushed his way into the room.

He glanced at her, his eyes crinkling in the corners at the sight of her.

He turned back to the door. "We'll need you in here," he whispered to someone outside. "They're chained."

A woman slipped through the narrow gap, and then Theo propped the door closed. Hopefully, if Marchant looked across at his prison, he wouldn't notice the door had been forced.

"Melodie." Caro gave a little wave. "Thanks for the rescue."

Everyone seemed a little . . . embarrassed at the sight of her, and Viviane wondered what had happened to make them all feel guilty.

Melodie didn't seem to hold any grudge, though. "Let's see," she said, crouching beside Caro to look at the rough keyhole.

She lifted Caro's ankle, angling it into the sunlight coming through the window.

"The key is square-shaped, and the end is short and bent at a right angle to the part he holds." Jon had been watching their rescuers with a face that tried not to show too much hope. "If that's what you're trying to understand."

Melodie looked over at him. "That's exactly what I'm trying to understand." She lifted her bag over her head and set it down, along with the small cup Viviane had noticed she was holding. She pulled out a piece of paper, and then a brush and a wooden box. She set the paper over the key hole and gave it a light rub, then opened the box to reveal watercolor paints, and began painting in quick, sure strokes.

Theo stood near the door, sword drawn, as if this was their usual method, his gaze flicking to Melodie every now and then, as if to make sure she was safe.

"What else would work, if this doesn't fit?" Melodie asked as she set the paper in a patch of sunlight. "Maybe a hand tong?"

As she said it, she pulled out another piece of paper and began to paint something on it.

While she was busy doing it, Theo stepped to the painting she had left to dry, plucked up what looked like a key that had suddenly appeared on it, and tried to open Caro's shackles.

"Too small," he said.

"I was afraid to make them too big," Melodie answered, grimacing. "It will take time to get it exactly right."

She set the second piece of paper in the sun, took the now blank page she'd drawn the key on and began to paint something else.

Theo had moved from Caro to Ivan, and tried to insert the key into his shackles. "No." He pulled back in frustration, and then lunged at what must have been a hand tong, not that Viviane had ever heard of one, or even seen it.

"Brace," Theo said to Ivan as he inserted the tongs into the shackle on his left ankle. He widened the handles.

The metal groaned as it was pushed outward, and with a final crack, it separated.

Theo bent to Gallain's ankle, but as he did, Vivi saw the hand tong wisp away to nothing.

Theo turned, as if there was no doubt there would be a replacement for him, and plucked it off its resting place on the paper, just as Melodie placed another painting in the sun.

"She makes it real, and then it disappears." Genevieve's words were hushed.

Theo had got Gallain free when they all heard the crunch of footsteps on the gravel.

"He just needs to look at the broken door to know I'm here," Melodie whispered. "It won't be a surprise." She pointed behind the door. "Hide."

Theo shook his head. "We both hide. I'm going to cut him down."

She gave a nod, and Vivi saw she'd been packing away her magic painting set, and as she moved to stand up against the wall behind the door, she folded a shirt over the top of her bag, covering the contents completely before she closed the flap.

Theo stepped in front of her, blocking her body, his sword raised.

His face was grim and his expression was flat.

But Marchant saw the door was broken before he even reached it.

"Who's in there?" he called out.

Theo shook his head to tell them to all keep quiet.

"Is it you, little girl?" Marchant's voice was a mix of excitement and fear. "Is it you breaking down my door?"

Everyone remained absolutely still.

Viviane saw Melodie and Theo exchange a quick look with each other, and she guessed Melodie had already had a run-in with Marchant. And come out of it unscathed.

He was frightened of her.

"You want to lure me in, but I'm not going to do that." Marchant's voice was sing song.

The silence stretched out.

Genevieve reached out and grabbed Vivi's hand, and a quick glance told her the boys looked as tense as she felt.

The four soldiers had risen to their feet, and Ivan and Gallain were loosening their shoulders, readying for a fight.

Marchant wouldn't last a moment if he stepped through the door, and Vivi guessed he suspected as much.

"I know the prisoners are still in there. You don't have a key to their shackles and there's no way you could have freed them all since I was last in there. So I'm going to make a deal with you."

"I wouldn't trust a deal with him under any circumstances," Jacinta murmured, and Vivi had to agree.

There was going to be no fair play here.

"The key and free passage for your friends, in exchange for you, little girl." Perhaps their silence had emboldened Marchant, because he sounded more sure of himself now. As if he imagined them in here, frightened and huddling. "I'll give you a few minutes to consider my offer."

The sound of boots on gravel told them all he was leaving, or at least moving away.

The moment he began to retreat, Melodie was crouched on the floor again, painting. The first of her hand tongs had just shimmered into existence when the *crunch crunch* of the stones alerted them to Marchant's return.

Theo's arms bunched as he snapped Caro's shackle, then he took up position as protector as Ivan grabbed the next one, and began working on Jacinta's ankle.

Theo crouched and tried to look through a crack in the door for some clue as to what Marchant was doing, and after a moment he swore, and jerked back.

"He's run up to the corner of the building and set something up against it." He moved to the door again, and when he turned to look at Melodie, his mouth was a grim line. "I think he's setting up some kind of magical barrier in an arch around the building, corner to corner, and . . ." He put his eye to the crack in the door again. "Three more in a semi-circle."

Melodie finished a hand tong painting, set the paper in what was now a much narrower strip of light, and stepped up to the door. She leaned against Theo, and Vivi saw his arm come around the back of her legs, as if supporting her.

But she didn't really need support.

Vivi's mind turned it over.

Maybe he just liked touching her.

She *was* beautiful. Her hair fell in a thick plait down her back, dark, glossy brown with fine threads of gold and red woven into it, and she radiated competence and intelligence, two things Vivi knew that Theo found almost irresistible.

"Whatever it is, it's spelled." Melodie shrugged without turning around. "I mean, he wouldn't be bothering otherwise, would he?"

"No," Theo sighed.

"What's the proposal, old man?" Melodie called out.

Vivi saw Theo's grip on Melodie's leg tighten, and then he forced himself to open his hand. He lay the flat of his palm against her thigh.

Melodie glanced down at him. "No choice. The tongs won't get the children out of the cell."

"He can't be trusted." Gallain was rubbing his ankle.

"I know." Melodie stepped back.

"I thought my little fence would force you to speak." Marchant chuckled. "The proposal is, you give yourself into my hands, and I'll let the others go."

Melodie turned her head so her voice would carry through the door. "The counter proposal is you let the others go, and then I give myself into your hands."

"Why would I agree to that?" He sounded so smug, Vivi wanted to hit him in the face the way he had hit her.

"Because every moment I'm in here, and you are standing watch out there, is another moment the Kassia and Cervantes army draws closer to Warven." She leaned against the wall near the door so he could hear every word she spoke.

Marchant was silent for a few minutes.

"The whole army?" He sounded like he was trying out the words on his tongue.

Melodie laughed. "After the horrors of the Chosen camps, what did you think the reaction was going to be from the Turncoat King when four of his baby soldiers were snatched?" She clicked her tongue. "Maybe you weren't thinking at all."

There was another silence, and Vivi didn't know if it was her imagination, but she thought it was electrified.

"Who would have even known they were gone so soon?" he asked at last.

"You know who, stop stalling, old man. There were two of us who came into Warven the night you took my colleagues around the camp fire. And your spy, who I followed here from town, already told you one of us left at first light this morning, headed back to Illoa. We were just the advance guard. For our children, we would burn down the world. Don't you remember that from the days of the Rising Wave?"

"Let's say all that's true, they won't find me here."

"Oh, they will. You're forgetting your box of nightmares is no more." She slid another painting into the sun. "I destroyed it."

Melodie stood and walked to the door.

She shooed Theo back, out of sight, and leaned out a little, so Marchant could see her.

"You miscalculated, old man. And the longer you pretend there isn't a ticking clock above your head, the better for me, so get back to me when you have a plan to do things my way." She stepped back, and Theo pulled her to the side, one of his big hands curled around her slim upper arm.

Vivi thought he was holding himself back, as if he wanted to pull her close in a hug.

"You aren't giving yourself up to him," he said.

"If it means getting the children free, I am," she said. "It's not as if I don't have a few tricks up my sleeve."

Theo closed his eyes, and Vivi thought he was going to say she wasn't giving herself up, no matter what, but after a beat, he gave a nod of his head.

They were buying their safety for Melodie's, and Vivi didn't even know her.

"Who are you?" It was Ric who asked. "Are you from Kassia and Cervantes?"

Melodie turned to look at them. "I'm a person who doesn't like people who steal children," she said. She stepped toward the door of their cell and Theo came with her.

She studied the lock, grimaced. "It needs to be precise, and that's just about impossible without the key, in which case I wouldn't need to paint it, anyway."

"At least paint some tongs to get them out of their shackles," Caro said.

Ivan lifted a shoulder. "It was hard for me to do. I don't think they'd have the strength to do it."

"Let's try another crowbar," Melodie said, and went back to her paints and paper.

"I'm ready to talk." Marchant's voice sounded tight and unhappy.

"Just a moment," Melodie called back, her brush giving a final flick before she shoved the page away and stepped back to the door. "Yes?"

"I let the children go, then you give yourself up, then I let the soldiers go."

"You let everyone go, and then I give myself up. The only details we have to discuss are how we accomplish that." She stepped away.

Ivan and Theo had wedged the crowbar between the door and the bars that made up the front wall, and with a surprisingly loud pop, the door snapped inward.

"What was that?" Marchant's voice was steeped in suspicion.

"That was me freeing the children from their cage, old man." Melodie stepped back to the door. "Tick, tock."

CHAPTER 28

"MARCHANT DOESN'T KNOW you're here." Ivan glanced at Theo as he held one of the hand tongs Melodie had drawn. She was becoming extremely good at painting them.

Ivan snapped the shackles on Ric's left hand and just like that, all the children were free.

Theo felt a surge of satisfaction, despite the fact that they were cornered. Having his students in sight was infinitely better than wondering what was happening to them.

"Agreed. He thinks it's just Melodie in here with us. We need to work that to our advantage." Jacinta looked toward the door, then over at Theo. She'd had her arms around the girls as they watched Gallain and Ivan work on the boys' shackles.

Theo had been thinking about how to play their advantage. He looked over at Melodie. She was still on the floor, where she'd knelt to paint the tongs. Her heavy braid swung forward as she reached over to close the paint box. As she picked it up, Viviane suddenly threw herself off the bench onto the ground beside her.

"Wait." She put a hand on Melodie's arm, bent her head, and murmured something in Melodie's ear.

Melodie lifted her head, looked at the princess, then gave a nod. She laid out a sheet of paper and opened her paint box again.

"Have the thread ready," she said.

Vivi glanced over at Theo. "You have some loose threads in your coat."

Theo looked down, saw she was right. It probably happened when he had tumbled into the trap near Marchant's meeting place.

Vivi crouched at his feet, looking up at him. "Can I pull them loose?"

He nodded, a prickle of understanding spreading from the back of his neck, down his arms.

She was going to embroider something. Like her mother.

Her secret was going to come out.

She tugged at the ripped edges on the hem of his coat and pulled three or four long threads loose.

If he were to guess, she had just asked Melodie to paint her a needle, and sure enough, as soon as she had the long threads of dark gray in her hand, Melodie set a picture of a slim needle in front of her.

"Get Ric's shirt off him as carefully as you can," Vivi told Jon.

Jon frowned, wanting to ask why, but Theo glanced at the boy, gave a nod, and after a moment's hesitation he helped Ric lift the shirt over his head.

"What're you up to, Viv?" Ric coughed a little as he bent to get the shirt off, and Theo could see the dark bruising along his abdomen.

His fury rose up again, and he forced it down.

"I'm helping you." The moment the needle appeared on top of the paper, she snatched it up, threaded it, and grabbed the shirt Jon held out for her.

She turned it inside out and began to sew, moving in quick, sure stitches.

Melodie was busy with a second needle, and it was ready to go almost exactly when the first one disappeared.

"It's such a strange feeling," Viviane said as she rubbed her forefinger and thumb together. Then she was threading the new needle, humming something as she did it, and the tingle Theo felt earlier rose up again.

This is what the queen did.

This was magic.

"Get it back on." Vivi bit the thread off with her teeth and Theo just caught a glimpse of an image of some kind of plant before she turned it the right way around again. She handed it back to Ric. "Wear it right up against your skin."

Jon helped him, and no one said anything as he pulled the shirt over his head with a wince. It was the kind of silence that was full of unspoken questions, but no one uttered a word.

Melodie finished packing up the paints, and this time, she didn't bother wrapping them up and hiding them. She simply put them on the top of her things in her bag.

The significance of that wasn't lost on him, and when she looked up, as if she sensed his gaze on her, their eyes met.

"What is your strategy?" he asked her. He wanted to ask her not to do it, not to give herself up, but he knew it was the one sure way to get the children to safety.

She set her bag carefully against the wall and then peered out into the growing dusk. "I'm hoping it gets a little later before we reach a deal, so it's harder for him to see you in amongst the others in the dark," she said.

"I'm not going with the others." Theo spoke slowly. "He doesn't know I'm here. I'll stay behind. Everyone will leave who he knows about. You'll step out. He won't expect there to be another person still inside."

She stepped out of the doorway, squinted at him in the growing darkness. "The others won't know where all the traps are."

"We'll tell them. Right now." Theo wasn't going to bend on this.

He gestured all eight of them over. The children needed to understand the danger just as much as the adults. He told them about the trap on the path from the workshop to the forest, the pit near the clearing, the spider's web over the road, told them how to avoid each one.

"When you get past the clearing, just climb straight over the fence as you step off the path onto the road, and follow it until you get to the gate. Nena is the farmer who owns the land. I don't think she's dangerous to you."

"Gus was ordered to stay with her for a few days before he goes back to the inn to spy on whoever comes from Illoa to look for the children," Melodie said. "He's probably gotten his things from the inn and moved in there by now. And he isn't compliant any more."

"Did Marchant give him anything else magical to use?" Theo asked.

She shook her head. "Not that I saw. I think he was supposed to watch and listen, then report back. But he is dangerous and he will run to Marchant if he sees you."

"That might not matter, but if he does approach you, be wary, and if you have to deal with him, so be it." Theo felt nothing for the man who had sold his soul to Marchant.

"The town guards, or some of them, are in Marchant's pocket as well. I'd avoid town altogether." Melodie worried her bottom lip as she spoke.

"Agreed. Marchant has our horses and our packs, though." Gallain rubbed the back of his neck, as if still discomforted by that.

"I'll get the horses he took and the packs as part of the exchange," Melodie said. "We found Caro's horse and it's at the inn, along with our own, so one of you will need to go get them."

Caro gave a nod. "And then we'll wait for you just outside town."

"No." Theo was shaking his head, and Melodie was doing the same. "Go. Just go as fast as you can with the children. There will be an army coming to meet you. Wait until the children are completely safe before you come back."

All of them looked like they wanted to argue.

"This is not a discussion. I am in charge, and those are my orders." Theo held each one of his team's gaze before moving on to the next.

All of them lowered their eyes and nodded.

"It feels like we're running away, like cowards. Saving ourselves with your sacrifice." Viviane spoke softly, and her friends murmured their agreement.

"You aren't soldiers yet," Theo pulled Vivi into a hug. "You are not responsible for anything that happened here. And the best way you can help me is by following orders and getting to safety. The thing that has held me back is worrying about all of you. Knowing you are far from Marchant, and he cannot hold your wellbeing over me, is all that I need."

She tightened the hug, and he ran a hand over her braided hair.

"Trust me. Trust me and Melodie to end this."

"I'm back, little girl." Marchant's voice was sing song. Theo wondered if he was spiraling into some kind of madness. His behavior was strange, to say the least.

He didn't like the thought, because at least a sane man was predictable.

"I'm here, old man." Melodie walked to the door. "What's your proposal?"

Gallain exchanged a look with Theo at her sarcasm, and Theo could see the appreciation in the soldier's eyes.

It was a reflection of his own.

"Apologies for the delay, I went to fetch a rope. I'll throw it toward the door. You put your hands through the loops I've already made in the rope and one of the soldiers can tighten them."

"And why would I do this?" Melodie asked.

"Because once you do, I'll move one of the stones so that your friends can get out. Once they are all out, I'll let you watch them run for the forest, and then you come to the gap and let me grab the rope."

"Afraid I'll throw the compliance net on you otherwise?" Melodie scoffed.

He paused. "Yes. And if you give it to one of your friends, I'll notice, and there will be consequences."

"He's delayed until dusk so he can see any magical items we may have." Jacinta spoke softly. "He thinks he's been crafty."

"Fine." Melodie pushed the door open a little wider. "But you'll have their packs and horses brought, as well. And throw the packs at the door along with the rope, so I can check you haven't secreted any nasty surprises inside."

"You'd be able to tell, would you?" Marchant asked.

"Yes, old man, I would be able to tell." Melodie's eyes closed, and Theo saw her throat work as she gave up her secrets to their enemy. As she made herself irresistible to him.

"I have no use for the horses or the packs, so I agree."

Melodie swung her bag over her shoulder and stepped out, and Theo bet Marchant salivated at the sight of her, all lit up with magic—her own and the spell-worked items she carried.

"The horses and packs," she said coldly, and Gallain and Caro stepped out behind her.

"He can't take his eyes off her," Caro murmured to Theo from his place pressed up against the wall beside the door. "He's moving to the stables, but he keeps looking back, like he can't believe his luck."

"Remember all the places we told you about where there are traps," Theo reminded Ivan and Jacinta as they headed out of the door themselves. "And there may be others, so avoid the forest, use the main road as much as possible."

"We'll get them out." Jacinta clapped her hand on his arm. "We won't let you down."

Vivi said nothing, she just gave him another hug, and Genevieve did the same. The boys tapped their chests with a fist as they went by, and Ric really did look like he was moving more easily.

Theo saw he kept rubbing the spot under his shirt where Vivi had put the embroidery.

Theo heard the sound of a horse whinnying, and a few thumps.

He wished he could see what was happening, but one of their few advantages was the fact that Marchant didn't know he was here and he couldn't risk being seen.

"Nice try. You wanted an early test of what I can do?" Melodie asked, voice dripping with scorn.

"Can't blame me for it, can you?" Marchant couldn't contain a cackle of delight. "Wait—" His shout was outraged as Theo heard a crack of something breaking.

"Oh, you wanted me to treat the nasty things you tried to hurt my friends with carefully, did you?" She didn't even try to sound sorry.

"My mistake," Marchant said.

Theo worried about his tone. It promised retribution.

"Yes, it was." Her answer was cheerful, as if oblivious to his fury.

He bet she wasn't oblivious at all, but he could do nothing about it but keep silent. And wait for his chance to kill the bastard.

CHAPTER 29

MARCHANT WAS incapable of hiding his glee at the sight of her.

Melodie could see the way his eyes turned to her over and over, even though he tried to keep an eye on the others as well.

He wasn't doing a very good job of it.

She picked up the rope he'd tossed into the semi-circle along with the packs, careful to avoid the pieces of clay she had smashed, and the white stuff that had spilled from the vessel.

They still exuded a glimmer of spell work, slimy and rotten.

She'd gagged as she'd lifted the small pot of what looked like salt out of Gallain's pack. She could tell it was poison, but she didn't have time to work out the effects. It didn't matter, this would not harm anyone else.

Her smashing it had given Marchant a real shock. He hadn't considered the danger of putting something harmful into the packs, only the benefits. She bet he'd smugly decided that the results would either be that he poisoned his prisoners, or that he found out if she could really see what it was.

He hadn't counted on finding out what she was capable of doing in more ways than one.

"Put your hands in the loops." Marchant was almost dancing

with excitement at the edge of the rock barrier. He was leaning on a stick, and it glowed.

She looked at the rope carefully, but there was no magic woven into it. It was a plain, unspelled rope. It was just going to be difficult to get out of once it was tightened.

She had taken the handkerchief, which held the few leftover sparkles from the box in the forest, out of her pocket before she had gone outside to confront Marchant, and had tucked it up her sleeve, where its very faint glow of protection would not be seen.

She lifted the rope up and put her hands through the loops, and felt a sudden weight in her chest, making it hard to breathe.

She had spent her life being quiet, helping from the shadows. Now she was standing in the spotlight, helping her enemy bind her.

Nausea burned in her throat, and she swallowed it down.

"Open a path," she said, lifting her arms to show him the loops were over her wrists. "Caro will stay back and tighten them when everyone else is through."

Caro moved to her side, standing with her stoically as they watched Marchant move the white stone that touched the left side of the building. He set it down a little way away.

"That stick is magic." She kept her voice low as she turned to the others. "It might be what he used on Ric."

They nodded in understanding as Ivan, Gallain and Jacinta picked up their packs and the children's packs, Ivan slinging two over each shoulder.

She knew they were looking for a way to attack Marchant as they left, she could read it in their body language, but if they failed to take him, if he had his usual array of tricks up his sleeve, all this negotiation would be for nothing.

"Just focus on getting the children away," she warned softly.

She saw Ivan hesitate, then finally give a nod.

"I'm not generous enough to return your cloak, girlie." Marchant flicked a hand at Viviane. "Thank your aunt of the north for me, won't you?"

"You should hope I do not so much as mention your existence

to her, old man," Viviane said, using the term of disrespect he seemed to like right back at him. "You would not want her to turn her attention, or the attention of her husband, your way."

"Maybe, maybe not." He rubbed his hands together, his face twisting in what might have been a smile, and Melodie wondered, not for the first time, if there was something wrong with him.

He had brought over three horses, and they looked like the ones from Illoa. One danced a little, as if nervous or disturbed, and Melodie caught the briefest glimpse of a glow.

"Stop." She raised her voice and everyone stopped, obeying her without question. She very deliberately let the rope loops slide off her hands onto the ground.

No one had yet gotten through the semi-circle.

Marchant's gaze went to her, and then he frowned at the sight of the rope on the floor.

"Get whatever it is you put under the saddle of the middle horse out. Show me what it is and then put it down." She should have known he'd try to play dirty. It was the only way he played.

"Well, well. This *is* interesting." He tried to sound calm, but he wasn't. He was thrilled and disappointed at once.

He moved to the horse, loosened its saddle and lifted it, slid out a small piece of cloth and put it carefully in his pocket. Melodie saw he was wearing gloves.

"Thank you," Caro whispered. "I bet whatever that was, it was nasty."

Melodie nodded. "Be so, so careful, and don't wait. Don't sleep. Just ride."

"We will." Caro's words were a vehement promise.

"Rope, or no one goes." Marchant waved his hand at her, and Melodie bent and put the rope loops over her wrists again, waggled her hands.

Gallain went first, sliding carefully along the wall for a few steps and then turning to keep an eye on the others coming through, as well as watching Marchant.

One by one the children made it through, and then Ivan and Jacinta walked out, grabbing the horses by their trailing reins.

"Now your turn." Marchant smiled.

"I hate this." Caro walked with her to the exit point and stepped on the boundary. Melodie held her hands out to her, and she pulled the middle piece of rope down and the loops tightened around her wrists.

Her hands came together, and just to test things, she slid her left hand down her right sleeve and touched the handkerchief with her fingertips. It settled her.

"Go." She watched Caro turn, run to grab one of the horses from Jacinta, and then they sprinted toward the forest, avoiding the path with the trap on it.

"You see the trap?" Marchant asked. "You told them about it?"

"I see everything, old man," Melodie said. "Everything." She looked directly at him, and then away, her sense of exposure excruciating.

"You see something on me, don't you?" Marchant's voice was soft but urgent. "What is it?"

She didn't see anything on him, but she didn't think he was testing her or lying. She didn't know what he was talking about.

"You must surely know." She judged that the most prudent response, and then she ignored him, watching as Gallain reached the tree line and waited for the others, and then how, one by one, they disappeared into the shadows.

"Give me your bag before you step out," Marchant said, eyes gleaming in the last, fading light of the day. "I want to see how much of the magic is you, and how much you're carrying with you."

She studied him—how close he was to her, whether she could pull the handkerchief out quickly enough and loosen the knot to get the sparkles out before he noticed.

Now was the best time to do it, while the barrier was standing open, while he didn't even have hold of the rope yet. But the wind was blowing straight in her face and would surely snatch the sparkles away, and he was keeping a wary distance.

"Your bag." He had been leaning on the magic stick, but now he lifted it up.

She had seen Ric's bruises. She would find it harder to escape or overcome him if she was badly hurt, so with a sigh of regret, she bent, lifting her bag over her head, and let it drop to the ground at her feet.

She didn't know how this would go.

She had never thought she was magical. Seeing the magic of spell work wasn't the same as being magic.

But Marchant gasped, looking between her and the bag.

"I don't know which shines brighter." He bent forward and snatched the bag up, dancing back as if suspecting she was still dangerous to him.

"My paints." He lifted the wooden box out in wonder. "Where did you get this?"

"How do you think we knew were to come find you, old man?" she scoffed. "The trader who stole your goat and your paint box from you read through your letters as well."

Marchant stared at her in total shock. "I didn't . . ." His voice trailed away.

He didn't know he'd been robbed.

Perhaps he thought Theo in his goat form had taken the bag that contained the paint box and escaped. She could see how he would come to that conclusion with both of them missing.

"He saw the children, too, of course. That's why we knew we were on the right trail. And one of us went back to let the rest of the army know where you are." She smiled, and felt her heart soar when he took a step back at the sight of it. "The commander of the Rising Wave is very unhappy. Very, very unhappy."

"You've never met the commander of the Rising Wave," Marchant scoffed.

"What am I, old man? What role do you think someone like me would have in the court of Kassia and Cervantes? The commander and his queen sent their best magic users out with their best military units. Looking for the first children to be taken since the Commander destroyed the Chosen camps." She thought that sounded plausible. She wouldn't mind that future, actually.

He looked at her, and she stared straight back.

"You work for the court." He said the words carefully.

"I work for the court," she agreed. "And for the military, when they need me."

"And they know about me by now?" He pursed his lips.

"Your name, where you live. What you've been up to. Everything." She enunciated each word.

"I very much doubt everything," he said, utterly serious.

"Maybe not," she agreed. "But once they get here, and start looking around, it won't take long."

"They'll lose people," he said. "I have protections."

"They have people like me," she countered. "Do you think I'm the only one?"

He paused. "Yes." He clicked his tongue. "You went too far, little girl. I believe most of what you told me, but now you're just being ridiculous. In all my time actively searching for another like me, I've never come across a single one, until you. Maybe the Commander and his queen have other magic users. I've never heard so, but the shirts their soldiers wear confirms they do, and that's a well-kept secret. But another like you?" He shook his head. "You present me with a real conundrum."

"And what is that?" But she already knew what he was going to say. She saw it in his covetous eyes.

"You would fetch me so much money with a court, rich or poor —they'd pay whatever I ask for you. But equally, you would be so useful to me as to be priceless. Absolutely priceless."

"I'll only be yours for so long," she told him, keeping her fear of his words and intentions from her voice. "The Rising Wave is coming for you."

"The Rising Wave crested, broke, and has done nothing more than lap at Kassia's shores for the last fifteen years," he said.

"You think the original members of the Wave don't remember

why they rose up to begin with?" she asked. "You think the queen and her commander are so complacent?"

He didn't think that. She could see him trying to keep his hands from shaking as he held the paint box.

"Nice paint set, by the way," she said, prodding him with whatever she could. "It was handy in breaking the children and my fellow soldiers out from their restraints."

He looked down at the paints. "You used it?" The look he sent her was astounded. "You actually used it?" The last words were almost a screech.

"Why wouldn't I?" she asked. "I bought it from that trader fair and square."

He opened the box, squinting a little, like she'd had to do, because of the bright glow coming off it.

"The black is nearly finished." He sounded barely able to say the words.

She shrugged. "It takes a lot of black to draw hand tongs that snap shackles."

"I will kill you for this." He snapped the paint box closed.

She laughed at him, keeping the fear from her face. "No, you won't."

He seemed to try to get a grip on himself, then stepped closer to her. At the last moment, she saw him swinging the stick.

It hit her lightly in the side, with hardly any force at all given the angle and how far away he stood, but it seemed to reverberate through her, like she had been smashed into a wall.

She fell to the ground, unable to breathe, and at last he approached, grabbed up the rope, and crouched beside her.

"You're right, I won't. But I can make you wish I would."

CHAPTER 30

Unable to stand not seeing a moment longer, Theo crouched down as low as he could and peered out of the broken door.

Melodie lay just beyond the white stones, curled up on the ground and unmoving.

He tensed, hunting for Marchant in the darkness, and found him rolling a white stone back into place.

The arch was closed again and he was trapped inside.

Why had Marchant closed it? Did he know Theo was here?

Theo recalled the long moments he'd been exposed to view from Marchant's house when he'd levered the door open.

Marchant might have seen him and been chuckling to himself this whole time.

"You're heavy." Marchant stood over Melodie, shook his head, and hobbled toward the stables, leaving her on her own.

Theo weighed the risks of getting as close to Melodie as he could and asking her what Marchant had done to her, but he wasn't sure if she was conscious, or how long Marchant would be, so he held.

If Marchant didn't know he was here, now was not the time to give it away.

He was glad he had stayed put when Marchant came straight back out, pulling a cart behind him.

He maneuvered Melodie onto it, taking very little care with her, and then pulled her toward the workshop.

The spell worker had to stop a number of times to catch his breath, and each time he did, he stood with his hand in Melodie's bag, touching something inside reverently.

The paint box, if Theo were to guess.

At last they reached the workshop door, and Marchant pulled the cart inside.

Theo collapsed back inside the prison. He rubbed a hand over his face. He had never thought Marchant would keep the barrier closed after everyone was out. He'd been counting on sneaking out.

But Marchant hadn't once looked in Theo's direction, and Theo didn't think he had the self-control to play such a deep game.

So, perhaps they still had some element of surprise, but that did nothing to help Melodie—unconscious, vulnerable, and in the hands of their enemy.

MELODIE CAME BACK TO HERSELF SLOWLY, TRYING TO IGNORE the annoying tapping on her cheek.

"There you are." Marchant's face floated above her. He didn't look happy.

"I didn't go anywhere," she managed to say. She refused to cower to this despicable man. "You hit me with a spelled stick, remember?"

With a jolt she remembered the handkerchief, and slid her left hand down her sleeve.

Nothing.

Her hands clenched. It was gone.

She swallowed the bile of defeat that rose up in her throat and closed her eyes again.

"Looking for this kerchief?" He waved it in front of her face. "Clever to scoop the last of the magic from the box. Not clever to let it drop out."

She simply shook her head, eyes still closed. Nothing she said could change what had happened.

"Come on. Get up." He tapped her cheek a bit harder, and she jerked away, eyes squinting as she tried to focus. The light in the room was low, coming from a single sconce near the door.

She noticed the stick, though, leaning against the wall beside them. It no longer glowed, and as she shifted to get more comfortable, she realized she hurt in more places than just her side.

He'd hit her a few times after she'd fallen, it seemed.

He'd used it up.

"You were scared you'd gone too far," she whispered. "Weren't you, old man? You're so out of control, you nearly killed the one thing you've hunted for your whole life."

He drew back from her as if she'd struck him.

"You shouldn't have used the paints," he said.

"I didn't even know who you were when I bought those paints. And I used them to work out what they did."

"You knew later, though," he insisted.

"Sure, later, after I spoke with the trader again, I knew he'd stolen them from you. Do you not use things because they've been stolen from someone else?" She glared at him from under her half-slitted eyelids.

He breathed out, as if trying to get his temper under control. "I'd been looking for these paints for years. I knew they'd been made, and I tapped every source I knew trying to track them down before someone used them up."

"They're not that useful," she said, with a shrug. She wanted to ask him who had made the paints, and how he knew about them, but she didn't think he'd answer. "The painted items only last a few minutes."

"What?" He sounded incredulous. He shook his head. "No, no, no. That's not what I was told."

"Try for yourself. You'll see." She cautiously stretched out where she lay on the cold, hard floor. She winced at the pain, and tried to work out whether he had her chained to anything or whether she was still just tied up with the rope.

Then she wondered what Theo was doing. Was he out there right now, waiting for them to emerge?

The thought soothed her.

She wasn't alone here. She had to remember that.

And it seemed she was still tied up in rope, but nothing else.

It was better than the alternative.

"Show me," Marchant demanded. "Draw something. But don't use the black."

She waited for a moment, but when it was clear he wasn't going to help her, she sat up and used the wall to get her feet beneath her and pushed against it to stand.

"Stop being so dramatic. You'll recover." Marchant tugged at the rope, drawing her toward the table.

"You going to untie me so I can use the paints?" she asked.

"No." He looked bullish.

She wiggled her fingers. "Then you'll have draw something. Anyone can use it." She sat on one of the stools he'd set around his work table.

He had laid the box down and had it open.

He turned to her. "Paper?"

"In my bag." She didn't want him touching her things, but they were long past what she wanted.

He pulled out a page, turned it over to look at the design she'd sketched on the other side.

"Use the blank side," she said. "I had to make do with what I could find."

He grunted in assent, to her relief seemingly uninterested in the pencil sketch and what it might mean. If there was ever a chance she would go back to jewelry making, she didn't want him knowing anything about it.

He dug around and found the cup and brush, and sat looking down at the blank page. "I can't draw," he said.

She said nothing. She wouldn't help this man in any way.

Eventually he dipped the brush in water and dipped it in the blue. She watched with interest as he tried to paint a bird.

It was not well done, and when he was finished, he set the brush down and stared at the page expectantly. Then looked at her when nothing happened.

"It has to dry first."

They watched paint dry, and still, nothing happened.

"This is the set, you aren't lying," he muttered to himself, touching the wooden box. "It glows bright enough to blind."

He suddenly grabbed her by the jacket and yanked her closer. "What aren't you telling me?"

She sneered at him. "Old man, I had less information than you when I got this set, and I worked it out. Try again."

"I don't have time for this." He twisted her shirt at the collar, but his grip wasn't strong. If he was trying to choke her, he didn't succeed, other than to drag her so close, she could see the spittle on his lips.

He suddenly shoved her back, stood up, and walked to a table that held an assortment of items. He picked up a black leather pouch and hefted it in his palm, as if it were full of gold.

"I got this beauty at the same time I got the paint set," he said, lifting it up to show her. "And it came in handy when I was attacked on my way home."

She wondered if whatever was in the pouch was what Marchant had used against Theo to immobilize him before he turned him into a goat. She found there was room inside her for a little more fear.

"What is it?" she asked. Might as well hear the bad news.

He loosened the strings at the top, dipped his fingers in, and suddenly flicked the contents straight at her.

It felt as if ice coated her face, pushing into her nose, her mouth, sucking away all her air.

She lifted her bound hands to her throat in panic, trying to brush whatever coated her skin away, and then saw lights in front of her eyes as she crashed to the ground.

She fought for breath, trying to suck in some air, and a tiny trickle kept her from blacking out. With a high whistle she managed to drag in some more, and it got easier and easier.

When she could finally breathe normally again, she continued to lie on the ground, eyes closed, just happy that her lungs worked.

"How many times can you use it?" she managed to pant out.

He suddenly went still, and came to stand beside her. "It never runs out."

She smiled at the lie, which she could hear in his voice.

"Sure it can, old man." She coughed a little. "Just like the things you draw with the paint set last forever."

"Tell me where the curse is." Suddenly Marchant was crouched beside her. "Four months ago, someone sold me things that looked steeped in magic, but they faded so fast. And since I handled them, I've been ill. I think there was a spell on one of them to kill me off so I couldn't come looking for him, to deal in the usual way with people who cheat me."

"When did you work that out?" she asked, coughing again.

"A few days after I got home. I started to feel sick and then I saw the things I bought were almost completely faded." The whites of his eyes did look yellow, now that she was this close to them. "Tell me where the spell is, little girl."

"You want me to help you, yet you hit me, you take away my air. I'm doing nothing for you, old man." She pushed up to sitting. "Can't you see it yourself, anyway?"

His mouth thinned. "No. That's clearly part of the spell. I don't know how he did it." He brandished the now-closed pouch in front of her face. "I don't care if I use this up, I'll take your breath as often as I have to to get your cooperation. Now, where is the spell?"

She hesitated. She really didn't want to go through being suffocated again. But she wouldn't admit there was no spell on him. "You have to draw things that have a realistic chance of being found in the world," she said. "Not like that poor excuse for a bird you painted. Rope or string works well."

He sat back on his heels, wanting to argue about her decision to talk about the paint set, but also very much wanting to use the paint set.

He leaned on the wall to help him stand, which told her his injuries were still bothering him, and then he went over to the table, opened the box again and drew a squiggly line on the page.

By the time Melodie had gotten to her feet and walked over, it had dried.

Marchant exclaimed in delight when a piece of green string appeared.

"Start counting," she said.

He did, slower than she would have, and then lifted the page when it disappeared as if to check it wasn't hiding below.

"I was lied to." He tapped his fingers against the table. "You draw something."

She wiggled her fingers at him again, and he stood, indicated she sit in the chair, and once she had, he loosened one of the rope loops so she could slide her right hand free.

She pulled the paper toward her, and something made her draw a knife. Something hot, and dark, and vengeful.

Theo was probably out there, waiting to pounce as soon as the door was unlocked and opened, but just in case, she would deal with Marchant now.

Maybe it was because she used blue and yellow as the colors that he didn't realize the significance, but as soon as the knife appeared on the page she snatched it up, twisted in her seat, and stabbed him.

He screamed and threw the pouch at her.

She had already braced herself for him using it, mentally preparing herself not to panic at the lack of air, knowing if she took it slow, she would be breathing again.

But it felt like it took longer—whether it did or not, she couldn't say. She fell from the chair, clutching her throat again, and this time, the world went dark for a bit.

When she came back to herself Marchant was busy retying her hand through the loop.

"You will pay, you will pay." He was muttering it under his breath to himself, almost rocking back and forth.

She kept herself lax, and even when he shook her shoulder with a bloody hand, she pretended to be unconscious, until he slapped her, hard.

She groaned and looked up at him, saw he was holding a hand to his stomach, and blood was oozing from the wound.

"You do that again, I'll kill you. Doesn't matter how long I've been looking for someone like you. It isn't worth it if this is how you're going to behave."

She took a careful, full breath of air, and pushed away from him. "You're saying you wouldn't try to do everything you could to escape if someone took you? Someone who behaved the way you behave?"

He seemed utterly confounded by her question.

Self-awareness was not Marchant's strong suit.

"I need to heal up." He backed away, his face showing the strain, but instead of moving to the door, he went to the table and upended her bag. She got herself up to a seated position, and watched him paw through her things. "Let's see what you've got for me in here, and then I'll lock you down for the night."

He sorted her spare clothes to the side, and then lifted up first the remedies book and then the brooch. "This is it?"

"This is just what I found in the last few days of my hunt for you." She kept her tone derisory. "You think I haul valuable magical items around me while I'm on a mission?"

He grunted. "The book should fetch something. The brooch?" He flicked it away, and it skittered across the table and fell off it. "Useless."

"Maybe, but I always take everything I find. Sometimes things have a way of surprising you."

He slanted her a look. "Very seldom."

She shrugged. She hoped Theo had a nice surprise for him when they got out.

He pushed his chair back, and caught her watching him.

"What do you see?" he asked. "Where is the spell?"

She shrugged. "Why would I tell you?"

He gritted his teeth. "Because if I leave you in the prison, and whatever is eating me up gets its way, you'll be stuck there, with no one to feed you or get you out."

"And if I tell you, I give up my one advantage," she said. Might as well spin this out as long as possible. "And I'm the one with time, old man. Not you."

He stood, swaying a little. If his skin hadn't looked gray before she'd stabbed him, it definitely looked gray now. "We'll see what you say when you're starving and thirsty. I have some time, and despite your best efforts, I'm not going to keel over tonight." He sent her a nasty smile. "And if that doesn't convince you . . ." He put a hand on the table as if to steady himself, and then snatched up the pouch. "There's always this. Try anything while I walk you back to the prison and I'll put you down on the ground again."

She gave a tight nod and he grabbed the rope and pulled her to the door.

He stepped out, pulling her behind him, and as soon as she was out of the workshop she wondered where Theo was. He would have attacked by now if he could.

Her gaze went straight to the prison, and she suddenly noticed that the stones of the magical barrier were back in place. He hadn't left the gap open.

He must have done it while she was down on the ground after he hit her with the stick. Which meant Theo hadn't been able to get out.

She was suddenly short of breath again.

"Why did you close the stones again?" she asked, suddenly worried he'd done it because he knew Theo was in there.

He turned to smile at her. "As long as I keep them in their box or in line, they'll never lose power."

"So the barrier lost some power when you opened it to let the others go?" she asked.

He gave a laugh. "Sorry to dash your hopes, but no. I moved the last stone in the arch to let them out, so I break the arch and then reset it when I put it back, with minimal power loss. The stones keep up a strong barrier as long as they're in alignment. I've had them for years. They've kept many, many prisoners in. So think about that." He brought her round to the side of the building, and moved the stone with his shoe.

He waggled the pouch at her as he backed up, and she obediently stepped through. He rolled the stone back in place and sent her a nasty smile.

"You hurt me, and I'm going to take as long as I need to heal. Which means don't count on food or water any time soon." He turned and walked slowly back to his house.

She thought about reminding him that an army was on its way to him, that he didn't have time to lie around and heal, but decided to keep quiet. He seemed to ignore whatever it was he didn't like to hear.

Maybe he thought the others would become ensnared in one of his traps, or that either Gus or one of the town guards would stop them.

Or he was so far into his own reality, he simply refused to consider that his time might be coming to an end.

She turned and made for the prison door, pushing it open.

Hands grabbed her gently and pulled her in.

Arms came around her in the pitch darkness of the cell. "Are you all right?"

She buried her face in his chest, suddenly shaking. "I am now."

CHAPTER 31

THEO STRIPPED the rope off her, alarmed at her shivering.

"What did he do to you?" He tried to pull back, to get a better look, but as soon as her hands were free, Melodie hugged him and he stilled, letting her come in as close as she could.

"It doesn't matter what he did," she whispered. "What matters is I got the better of him."

"Of course you did." He ran a hand down the back of her head, smoothed her braid between her shoulders.

She chuckled against his chest. "You don't even know what I did."

"Whatever it was, it was magnificent," he said.

"I stabbed him. And I think I found out how we can break free." She lifted her head at last.

"You stabbed him?" Looking at her in the faint light coming from the window above, he saw blood smeared on her cheek. He wondered what price she'd paid for that, while he sat here, unable to do anything.

"He made me paint something. So I painted a knife and stabbed him with it."

He had to hold back a sudden shout of laughter. "He didn't think it was a bad idea to watch you paint a knife?"

"Somehow, not. And I hurt him, but not enough to put him down. And he . . ." She suddenly shivered. "He retaliated. But the main thing is what I got him to say about the stones. Reading between the lines, I think their power is dependent on them being in alignment. That's why he closed it back up before he took me to the workshop."

He stared at her, suddenly sick to his stomach about what that retaliation might have entailed, but she fisted her hands on his chest.

"If I understood what he was saying correctly, we just have to push any stone other than the last one out of alignment, and I think the barrier might eventually shut down."

Eventually could be any time, but he refused to mention it. He didn't have a plan to escape, so hers was the best they had. "So how do we move one out of alignment?" he asked.

"Let's go see." She pulled back. "I have an idea."

Theo stood in the doorway, leaning against the doorjamb, arms crossed, as she walked along the barrier, studying each of the stones in turn. It was better for them both if he stayed in the shadows and reduced the risk of Marchant seeing him.

She looked toward the house, studying it as carefully as she had the stones, and then gestured to him. "I think he's asleep, all the lights are off."

He walked over to join her, and she pointed.

"There's the line."

He saw it was a perfect semi-circle, and almost certainly something Marchant had done well before he'd ever kidnapped the children. This was part of his fail safe to keep his prisoners contained, and each stone sat on the very edge of the arch.

Melodie sat down, and then lay flat on her stomach, studying the rock at the apex of the curve. She extended her hand and tried to push it, but her hand bounced back as it encountered an invisible wall.

"Hmm." She rolled a little on her side, and looked up at him. "Do you have a short knife?"

She looked better than she had a few minutes ago. Beautiful and determined. She could have asked him for anything and he would have given it to her if he could.

"A knife?" she asked again, and he fumbled for the one strapped to his thigh, drew it from its sheath and handed it to her.

She twisted her lips in a grimace. "I'm probably going to ruin it."

He crouched beside her. "That's fine." He reached out and touched the smear of blood on her cheek.

"Thanks." She began using it like a spade, digging into the ground just in front of the stone, making an angled hole.

"You're going to try digging under the line?" he asked at last.

"I can see exactly where the spell begins and ends," she said. "So if I can come at the stone from below, I think I can nudge it out of alignment."

"But that won't give us enough room to escape," he guessed.

"No, but if Marchant was telling the truth about the energy leech, then we should see the strength of the barrier erode over time." She took a break from digging and looked up at him again. "And if it dissipates quickly enough, we could escape before he comes back."

"Let me take over for a bit," he said, lying down beside her.

They took it in turns, watching Marchant's house when they weren't digging.

"He thinks he's been spelled or cursed, you know." Melodie propped herself up on an elbow as she watched him dig.

Theo stopped. "Wouldn't he see it?"

She lifted her shoulder. "That's what I asked him, but he said it was part of the spell that he couldn't see it. He's convinced."

"And is he?"

She quirked her lips. "I don't think so. But I haven't told him that."

He liked the idea of Marchant worrying about being spelled. "What does he think it's doing to him?"

"Killing him slowly." She turned onto her stomach and went back to watching his house. "I think he really is sick, but people get sick all the time and no magic is involved. I wonder if he isn't looking for magical means because that's his frame of reference."

Theo didn't care. Marchant wasn't going to live long enough to die of illness or old age. He was going to make sure of it.

"I think I need to take over. We're nearly there." Melodie nudged him out the way and began angling the knife down and then upward, and Theo saw the stone move, just a little.

When it landed back in place, she set herself right over the hole, elbows holding her up as she scooped the knife down and then up a few more times, and finally the stone shifted just the tiniest bit.

She tried a few more times, but the small move had changed the angle, and she got no more traction.

"Hah." She lifted up off her stomach, leaning back on her heels, her rapt gaze fixed on something he couldn't see. "I'd like to have moved it a bit more, but the magic is wafting away. A golden spiral out and upward."

Her gaze flicked suddenly to the house. "If he looks out, he'll see it."

"Then we have to hope he doesn't look out." Because there was nothing they could do about it.

She sighed. "Yes. I injured him pretty badly. I think he's probably resting." She pushed to her feet, and he joined her.

For a moment they stood in each other's arms in the darkness, the stars fat and bright above them, the forest whispering around them, the cool air making everywhere they touched warm and comforting.

"What have we got here?" he asked her eventually, voice quiet.

She looked up at him, eyes big. "You need to tell me, soldier. I'm the sweet young woman who has no business with the likes of you."

He grinned at her repeating the words the trader had said the day they caught up to him. "You keep up just fine."

"Maybe." But her eyes cut away. "I've been locked away for a long time, Theo. My father was so worried I would be snatched, he hovered over me like a hawk. And then Vinest was so worried he'd lose his very cheap labor that he manipulated me into closeting myself away." She sighed. "I used to watch the Kassia and Cervantes soldiers in the square, laughing and joking, and feel so jealous. You know how to navigate the romantic waters. I'd just drown."

"You won't drown." He slowly maneuvered them back toward the prison, out of Marchant's line of sight. "I won't let you."

"That feels . . . uneven." She swung with him as they made it through the door, and he suddenly had her pressed up against the wall.

"Tell me how I can make it feel even."

She studied his face in the dim starlight that came through the window above her head.

"Do you really want this? I think I'm probably a lot of trouble." Her voice was so soft, and he thought he caught sadness in it.

"Who made you think that?" He leaned closer and felt a quick stab of desire when she set her face in the crook of his neck, her lips against his collarbone.

"I'm sure Vinest hinted it, but I knew not to listen to him. I think it's more that there are a lot of complications when it comes to me. If I use my skills, I'm a target. If I don't use my skills, I'm a rotten person." She lifted her head. "I've been working in the shadows, and not doing everything I could do. I feel like a failure."

"You were on your own. You have a right to protect yourself. When this is done, come back with me to Kassia and Cervantes, and you can help people with my sword at your back." He would make the Commander see the benefit of it, or he would leave the army.

She raised her hands and held his face between his palms. "You mean that?"

"I mean that."

"That's a lot." She kissed his cheek and he slid his fingers into the back of her braid, cupping her head.

Then he lifted her up, turned and leaned back against the wall, so she was the one crowding him.

"What's this?" she asked, and he could see the flick of nerves as she wet her lips, but she pressed against him, and carefully pushed his hair back from his forehead.

"It's whatever you want it to be," he told her.

"This is you, letting me even up," she said. And then she pressed her lips against his.

He hadn't intended for anything to really happen between them. Marchant was just a field away, and still very much a threat, but her kisses were so sweet, and everywhere she touched stoked the fire in him even hotter.

Eventually, he had to set her away.

"I need to keep my wits about me." He straightened with a wince and then pulled her back in his arms, unwilling to lose the heat and scent of her. "Let's just turn it down a bit."

She snuggled close, and ran her hand up and down his back. "Thank you."

"What for?"

"For making sure I didn't drown." She sighed contentedly.

"Sweetheart," he told her, absolutely serious, "I'm the one floundering now."

CHAPTER 32

VIVIANE WATCHED as Gallain and Ivan used raw strength to knock down the fence posts right opposite where they'd come off the path.

Marchant's compound was behind them, and they had negotiated the woods below his house and gone through the clearing with the bell, so far without anyone falling into a pit or dying some terrible, magic-induced death.

She knew her nerves were near snapping point, and the way Gallain and Ivan attacked the fence, she guessed she wasn't the only one.

The horses hadn't liked the narrow path and were happier to be out in the open, but Melodie and Theo had stressed there was a trap along the track that ran beside the fence, and the horses weren't going to jump over it, so it had to come down.

"Hey! Hey, what are you doing?" A woman walked across a barren field toward them with a lantern lifted over her head. She appeared to be unarmed, but Viviane could see a man just behind her, keeping a little back so he was almost invisible in the shadows.

This must be Nena, the woman who owned the land that Theo

had told them about. Viviane couldn't blame her for being alarmed at her fence being destroyed.

Caro and Jacinta moved forward, both with knives in their hands, leaving Gallain and Ivan to finish flattening the fence.

Marchant hadn't returned their swords, but all four of them had obviously had knives in their packs because they'd each found at least one as they'd moved through the forest, and now wore them at their belts.

"Soldiers?" Nena stopped in surprise.

"You steal children from Kassia and Cervantes, you get soldiers," Caro said. Her voice was soft, but even Viviane shivered at the tone.

"No, I didn't steal . . ." Nena's gaze went to Vivi and the others, holding the horses' reins on the track. "Marchant." She said his name bitterly. "But why not use the track?" she asked, the heat gone completely from her voice.

"There's a trap on the track," Jacinta told her. "It warns Marchant who's coming and going."

"What do you mean, a trap?" The man finally got closer to Nena, so he was visible in the light from her lantern.

"A magical spiderweb built across the track. Every time you walk through it, Marchant knows." Caro's body shifted slightly, keeping the man directly in front of her.

He swore, the sound low and angry. "Did you know?" He turned to the woman.

She reared back and took a step away from him. "Did I *know*?" Her voice dripped with disdain. "I have barely been capable of tying my own boots for the last few years, and given how clear my mind is now, I'm betting you and Marchant had something to do with it."

"Sorry." He half-lifted a shoulder in a defensive move. "Of course you didn't know."

"You're Gus?" Ivan joined Caro and Jacinta, while Gallain moved toward Vivi and the others, gesturing for them to walk the horses over the fallen fence.

The man flinched, and Vivi, carefully and slowly guiding a horse over the wooden planks, guessed from his reaction that he was.

He lifted both hands, and she saw he was holding a knife in one of them. "Gus?" he asked, trying for casual.

"He's Gus," Nena said. "Marchant's faithful servant."

"That's a problem," Caro said. "We understand you're very likely to scurry off and let Marchant know we came this way. We aren't going to let that happen."

Gus spun, and bolted across the field.

Caro lifted her knife, her movements smooth and unhurried, and threw it.

With a strange half cry, half shout, Gus went down.

Ivan and Caro looked at each other, then jogged over to him.

Jacinta stood where she was, watching Nena.

But Nena had turned, and slowly walked after them, Jacinta shadowing her.

Caro pulled her knife out of Gus's back, and he made another sound.

So he was obviously still alive.

"Theo and Melodie said you were probably no friend of Marchant." Caro turned to Nena as she stood beside them, looking down.

Nena gave a laugh, and shook her head.

"Then we have a proposal. We'll tie this one up for you, and ask that you keep him until we send someone back to fetch him. We're talking at the most a week, hopefully less. And Kassia and Cervantes will pay you for your trouble, and make restitution on the fence."

Nena stared at her, head angled to the side. "That's the most fair anyone's dealt with me for years." She held out her hand. "It's a deal."

They stood in the cold, shivering a little while Ivan, Caro and Jacinta carried a weeping, pleading Gus into what looked like an old stable. They were probably only gone for half an hour, but as the darkness gathered in the woods behind them, and the air got colder, it felt like time stretched out, that Marchant could have dealt with Melodie and was right now running after them, terrible spells at the ready.

Nena came back with the three soldiers, talking softly.

"I can show you where the horses are kept at the inn," she said as they came into earshot. "Maybe save you some time?"

"I'll go with you." Jacinta flicked a look at Gallain and he gave a tiny nod. "We know the town guards have a deal with Marchant, so we need to be invisible."

"I know the guards." Nena sounded bitter. "I didn't know they were in with Marchant, but that makes a lot of sense." She drew in a breath and flicked a quick look at Vivi and her friends. "I'll be a diversion if you need one."

"Appreciate it." Gallain kept all suspicion from his voice, but none of them trusted her completely. Still, if she was being sincere, she could help them ghost through town.

She led them out of her gate and down the track toward Warven, with Jacinta sticking close to her.

The night was almost completely silent except for the sound of the horses hooves on the hard-packed ground and the rustle of clothing.

Viviane let herself believe, for the first time since they ran for the forest, that they might actually be free. Her eyes watered, and her nose started to run, and she slid her pack off her shoulder and found a handkerchief inside.

It was one her mother had embroidered for her, and she gripped it tight in a white-knuckled fist. She felt the tingle of her mother's magic, and dabbed away her tears.

"It's starting to feel real, isn't it?" Ric hooked an arm over her shoulder, his voice soft. "And once we're free and clear, we need to talk about what you did to my shirt. To me."

She glanced over at him. "No, we don't."

He stared at her, his expression thoughtful. "I think we do. But we have time." He dropped his arm, but kept close to her, walking shoulder to shoulder.

"Ric—"

"It's all right," he murmured. "This is just between you and me."

She relaxed a little. "As long as you understand that."

Up ahead, beyond a line of trees, the night sky lightened with the glow of a small settlement, and Gallain looked back at them, finger to his lips.

They fell silent, and Jacinta and Nena disappeared, running ahead.

"We go this way," Gallain whispered. "Nena says there's a short cut through the woods to the main road."

"And do we trust her?" Viviane asked.

"No." Ivan suddenly loomed out of the darkness, and Viviane realized he'd been scouting ahead. He was holding his knife in a very businesslike manner. "But it does look like there is a short cut. I'll go ahead, whistle if it's clear."

Caro had fallen back, taking up the rear, Vivi noticed. Gallain had already moved to the front.

They were getting out of here. They were really getting out.

CHAPTER 33

MELODIE WATCHED the magical barrier erode, little by little.

At one point, deep into the night, she wondered if it would dissipate fast enough to be of any use, but it clearly reached a tipping point sometime after midnight, and a few hours later, it winked out completely.

"Time to go." She glanced inside at Theo, a dark, reassuring figure in the shadows, and gave herself a moment to admire him as he straightened to his full height.

"It's down?" He pulled his sword from the scabbard at his back, and she could see the hardness in his expression.

She nodded, for the first time confronting what was about to happen.

They were taking the battle to Marchant this time. And there was no mercy in Theo's heart.

Or her own, come to that.

But they had both agreed it was better to take him alive, to get some idea of how many people he had taken through the years, and where they were.

The Commander could decide what happened to him after that.

"I hope he kept records," she'd told Theo as they'd discussed it. "I'd trust that more than anything that comes out of his mouth."

Now the time had come to find out.

She walked across the grass, Theo by her side, and nothing stopped them as they stepped over the boundary.

Marchant's house stood dark and quiet, and they both stopped at the foot of three rickety stairs that led up to a small porch at the front of it.

Melodie studied it carefully. There was no sign of spell work anywhere, and finally she glanced at Theo and gave a nod.

Then they circled around to the right. They'd already decided it was best to know all the surprises before they went in.

There was nothing that she could see, though.

Maybe having too many magical traps was annoying to work around for Marchant. He had been running this operation for a long time by the looks of things, and had gotten away with it so far, and he was arrogant enough to think he was untouchable.

Theo had checked the windows, which were all closed, and the back door, and they'd gotten an idea of the size of the cottage and how many rooms it had.

Eventually, they decided to go through the back door, which had a single stone step up to it, rather than the creaky planks that waited for them at the front.

Theo tried the door, and it opened with a faint squeak under his hand.

He froze, and then slid through the narrow opening, and Melodie followed him.

There was no light, except what came in with them from the night sky, and they both stood in the kitchen, listening carefully.

The room smelled of toast and tea, with an underlying, greasy odor that made Melodie's nose twitch.

Theo's hand came back to grab hers, and he began to move through the small room into the passageway that ran the length of the house.

She could just make out the front door at the end of it, and there were two doors on either side, all closed.

Theo indicated he'd check the rooms to the left, and so she went right, quietly turning the knob. The room within was a bathroom by the smell of mold and water, and a vial of spell-worked powder lent a glow to the small space.

She could see it was some kind of healing mixture, and she slipped it into her pocket. No doubt Marchant used it to help him heal from his wounds, and she wasn't going to let him have any more access to it.

She stepped out of the room, and Theo was waiting for her. He had left the door behind him open, and in the faint light from outside, she could see a couch and she smelled the ash and burned wood of a fire that had gone cold.

She moved down to the next door, in tangent with Theo, and then glanced behind her as she realized he was waiting for her to open her door, sword already half-raised. She swung it wide, looked inside, but it was empty of Marchant, although full of other things.

She stepped in, taking in the wink and glow of spelled items on shelves, and set in boxes on the floor and chair. Nothing was as bright as the paint set, but she had never seen anything as bright as that, except for the twine that had imprisoned Theo.

She heard a noise behind her, and spun around, but it was Theo stepping into the room.

"He isn't in the bedroom, either," he said, voice very low.

That seemed strange to her. Where else would he be but in this house? He was tired, sick, and injured, and she didn't think there was any other place for him to go.

"Do you think he's gone looking for the others?" That was a possibility. That he was checking his traps to see if he had managed to get the children and the rest of the team back under his control.

Theo gave a grim nod and stepped deeper into the room, and as he moved away from the door, she saw a glow of spell work, and then caught sight of Marchant, creeping up behind him, something with a metallic blade in his right hand.

The spelled glow was from a scarf around his neck, and she realized all at once that Theo couldn't see him. He probably *had* been in his room, lurking like the spider in his web.

"Careful!" It was the first thing that came to mind to shout out as she leaped forward, shoving Theo out the way to grab at the scarf.

With a hiss, Marchant shoved something at her with his left hand, and as she felt the ice cold against her face, felt the air sucked from her lungs, as she fell to the ground, she tried to remember that she could live through this.

She had done it before.

CHAPTER 34

Theo knew it the moment he saw Melodie's eyes focus beyond him, to the door. They had widened, and she moved, shoving him aside as she reached for something—

He turned toward her, slightly off-balance, and saw her fall, something clutched in her hand. Then Marchant appeared out of nowhere just in front of him, turned almost completely away to focus on Melodie.

He had done something to her, something that had her gasping for breath, and as she lay there, Marchant lifted a long, curved blade in his hand as if to strike her.

Time slowed, like Theo often found it did in a fight, his focus on his target absolute as he swung his sword in a controlled, powerful arc.

This would be a killing blow, but although they had discussed keeping Marchant alive, he had no regret in him as his blade found its target.

Marchant fell, and Theo beheaded him in a single, clean move to make sure he would never get up again, before he landed on his knees beside Melodie.

She was making strange, whistling noises as she struggled for air, and panic grabbed him in its tight, suffocating grip.

"What can I do?" He half-lifted her, but her eyes were closed as she concentrated on getting air.

"S'all right," she coughed at last. "Temporary."

He cradled her across his thighs as she got her breathing back under control.

"He did this to you, too, do you remember?" she asked.

"When I stabbed him?" He remembered falling down, but so much happened after that, he didn't have a clear memory. "How do you know?"

"He told me when he did this to me before. In the workshop."

Theo looked over at the body, and wished he could kill him again. Instead, he tightened his grip on Melodie and stood with her in his arms, then set her down on the far side of the desk, away from the blood.

She glanced across, shuddered, and tightened her hold on his sleeve. "Thanks."

"I wish I could do it again," he said, and meant every word of it.

"What now?" she asked.

He began to light the wall sconces. "Find everything related to who he stole, and who he sold them to, that we can, burn all the evil shit, and go."

She grimaced. "Then we'll be here for a while." She waved at the shelves. "Unless you class everything spell-worked as evil."

"It's all magical?" Theo eyed the shelves. They were poorly packed, and there were gaps where something had obviously been kept that was no longer there.

That worried him, made him wonder what it was Marchant had disposed of or sold on.

Melodie nodded. "Some of it might be useful."

He didn't want to admit that, but the invisibility scarf was definitely something he wouldn't mind having. He lifted it. "Can anyone use this, or was it specifically made for him?"

She shook her head. "It's from Skäddar, I can tell by the embroidery letters. It's probably an incantation to invisibility, so I'm guessing anyone can use it."

He put it on. "Now I'm gone?"

She grinned at him. "I can see you. But I could see Marchant, too. That's my secret power, remember?"

He tossed the scarf to her and she wound it around her neck and disappeared instantly.

"Now you're gone," he said.

She unwound it, handed it back. "I've seen this once before, on a woolen hat. But I can't remember the working. I don't think it was an incantation in lettering, it was an embroidered object." She went quiet, her eyes getting a far away look. "Telling eyes not to see." She smiled suddenly at him. "So there are at least two people who could make something like this."

"And you know one of them?" He thought she was accessing a memory. A pleasant one.

"Long ago, when I was little. Just before we moved from Kassia and Cervantes into Grimwalt."

"So you really are one of us," he said, liking the sound of it. "You're not Grimwaldian at all."

She shook her head. "No, although my father would never give me a straight answer about where I was born. He seemed to think it would be dangerous for me." She sighed. "He was frustrating in so many ways, and yet, he would do anything for me. Did do anything for me."

Her gaze went back to Marchant's body, and he realized it was bothering her a lot.

"I'll get rid of him," he said. "You start looking through the papers."

She nodded in relief, and he noticed she turned away when he picked Marchant's head up by the hair in one hand and grabbed the back of his coat with the other.

He went out the front door, and stood in the moonlit yard, wondering where to toss the body.

The prison was right in front of him, and Theo decided it was a sign.

CHAPTER 35

TURNING BACK WAS the hardest choice Ava had ever made.

She'd stepped away as Luc, Rafe and Lineka had questioned the frightened trader they'd roused from sleep at a small camp on the Taunen road, and stitched a quick truth seeking into the strip of cotton she always kept in her pocket. She'd pushed past Lineka and then squeezed between Luc and Rafe and held it out to the trembling man.

Luc had sent her a quick look as the trader had taken it, babbling his thanks as if she were gifting him a boon. He'd been so grateful, the sight of her a relief to him, as if he believed the hulking warriors crowding him would not harm him in her presence, when she would be the first to strike him down if he was lying about her child.

She'd questioned him while he'd held her spell work tight in his closed fist, and he repeated the same story.

A girl and some soldiers had already stopped him, and he'd told them to go to Warven.

Tiano had made a face when the four of them returned to the unit waiting on the road and gave her the town's name. She'd pointed back the way they'd come.

She'd accompanied them from the Illoa barracks. Captain Draper had offered them whoever they wanted as a guide, but Tiano had already proved herself and Luc had asked that she continue on with them.

"Back? How far?" Luc asked.

"The road that curved off to the right about three hours back." Tiano lifted her shoulders. "I've never been there, but I've been told it's small and out of the way. There's no through route to anywhere. It's a dead end."

"How far from where the road splits to the town itself?" Ava asked.

Tiano shook her head. "I'm not sure."

Ava exchanged a look with Luc.

"We go now," he said, holding her gaze.

He knew her. And she knew him.

There would be no sleep until they had Viviane back.

"Agreed." Lineka's voice was deep and a little hoarse. He'd been a quiet, steady presence the whole way, but now there was a real destination, he all but quivered.

They rode, hard and in silence.

At the turn, they slowed and then stopped, let the horses rest a little and allowed everyone to drink some water.

The moon was high, and in its silver wash of light, she could see no sign of farmland or any dwellings. There was a hill in front of them, dark with trees, and the road seemed to curve around it.

She felt restless, unable to settle, even though her mount needed the rest and she knew she should drink and eat something. But her baby was out there.

This was how her mother and father must have felt when she'd been taken by her cousin, Herron. How her grandmother and grandfather would have felt when her mother had been snatched as a young woman, as well.

It was almost intolerable.

She left her horse with one of the soldiers in the unit, and took her travel bag with her as she walked to the front of the group.

She stood, looking down the road, sipping from her water pouch. She sensed Luc behind her, and then she was enveloped by the warmth of his cloak as he stood at her back and pulled it around them both.

She leaned against his chest, and angled her head to look up at him, but he was watching the road in front of them, too.

She sighed. "I just want to have her back, and for her to be all right."

"I know." He tightened his hold.

She faced forward, and then frowned, trying to make out what she was seeing.

It looked like a group of people was traveling toward them, although she couldn't make out how many.

"Is that—?"

Luc turned and gave a whistle, and suddenly there was absolute silence as everyone focused ahead.

"It's a group of riders. It's unusual for them to be leaving the town this late." Luc gripped her under her arms, swung her around as he turned, and they both ran for their horses.

Everyone was mounted and waiting when the riders drew near enough that they could make out six horses.

One of the riders, the one in the lead, suddenly called out a hail.

"Gallain?" Tiano pushed forward on her horse. She gave a whistle, and it was answered by at least two of the people shrouded in darkness but getting clearer all the time.

"It's them." Tiano turned to her. "It's the unit from the barracks that went with Lieutenant Hallan."

Ava didn't wait. She began to ride toward them, and suddenly Luc was by her side, keeping pace as they galloped toward the small group.

"Mom!" The shout came from a rider in the middle of the group, and Ava tried to swallow a sob at her relief, hearing that voice.

"Vivi?"

They slowed as they reached the group, with Ava realizing the whole unit had caught up, surrounding the six horses.

She saw Vivi was sharing a mount with Genevieve La Rochal, and she pushed past the two soldiers leading the group to envelop both girls in a fierce hug.

"My baby," she whispered in Viviane's ear. "I was so worried."

Vivi gave a gurgling laugh, and was suddenly lifted off her horse into her father's arms.

Ava kept hold of Genevieve, and the girl put her head on Ava's shoulder and wept.

Beside her, she was aware of Lineka pulling his son Jon into a hug, then doing the same to Ricardo Bann.

"Where's Theo?" Rafe's question cut through the joy of the moment, and the small group went quiet.

"He stayed behind," Vivi said, voice soft. "Melodie swapped herself for us, that's how we got away, and Theo stayed behind to try to rescue her."

"Melodie?" Luc was holding Vivi like a baby in his arms, his piercing gaze locked on to the soldier who'd been riding lead in the group, the one Tiano called Gallain.

"She came with us from Illoa, Commander." Gallain dipped his head in respect. "Because of her . . . skills." He suddenly looked uncomfortable, but Ava knew about secrets, especially magical secrets, and didn't hold it against him at all. It made her like him even more.

"We heard about her from Captain Draper," she said, and he shot her a look of relief.

"Yes, well, Marchant, the man who took the children, wanted her, and she negotiated our release, in exchange for her allowing him to imprison her."

"He wanted her more than the children he'd gone to such lengths to kidnap?" Lineka sounded doubtful.

"Her . . . skills . . . were ones he'd been looking for, and he realized he'd made a mistake taking the children. We also managed to convince him there would be plenty of people looking for the children, that he would be better off letting us all go." One of the other soldiers spoke up, a woman with dark hair, who looked as disheveled as the rest of them did.

"Caro's right," Vivi said. "Melodie made herself irresistible to Marchant. I don't know if he thought he could snatch us again later, or whether he really was done with us, but he let us go, and tied Melodie up."

"And Theo?" Rafe asked.

"Theo was hiding with us, but Marchant didn't know he was there. So he was going to sneak out after we'd gotten away, and help Melodie escape." Genevieve sat up straight on the horse.

"The lieutenant ordered us to get the children to safety. To ride until we had them back with you, Commander," Gallain said.

"How far from us is this place?" Rafe asked.

"An hour's ride," Gallain said.

"There are magical traps." The soldier who had taken up the rear of the small group, a large man with broad shoulders and a slightly crooked nose, warned. "Corporal Ivan Sulaman, Commander." He put his fist over his heart. "Melodie told us where they were, and how to avoid them, but there could be more."

"Melodie." Ava felt something tighten in her. "How old is she?"

"Around my age," Caro said. "Early twenties."

That would fit. If it was the same Melodie. She had been five going on six when Ava had met her.

"The town guards are also untrustworthy," Ivan said. "They're in the spell worker's pay."

"He had the whole town spelled." The fourth soldier spoke for the first time. "Corporal Jacinta Allein, Commander." She repeated Ivan's move, with her fist over her heart. "Melodie destroyed whatever he was using to do it. We never had time to work out the details, but it clouded the townsfolk's minds until a few days ago."

"It clouded our minds," Gallain said. "That's how he captured us."

"But not Theo and this Melodie?" Rafe asked.

Gallain shook his head. "Luckily."

Luc looked around, then caught Ava's gaze. "I think we all need time to regroup, and rest. We'll set up camp right here until dawn, and then we pay Warven a visit."

A ripple of agreement went through the group.

No one wanted to leave this insult unchallenged.

Marchant had taken what he had no right to. And there would be consequences.

It would be a lesson to anyone who thought to take a child from Kassia and Cervantes.

There would be no mercy.

CHAPTER 36

MELODIE LEANED back against the wall of Marchant's house and dozed.

She had spent a half hour working through his papers, but she was bruised and exhausted. She refused to stay in the house to sleep, though. The smell of ingrained decay, as well as the blood Theo had spilled, chased her out into the cool air, and she'd eventually found a spot on the porch to rest for a bit.

"Do you want me to find you a blanket?"

She opened her eyes and saw Theo standing on the bottom step, looking up at her. He had washed himself off somewhere, perhaps at the water pump she'd noticed beside the stables, and his hair was spiky and wet.

She shook her head. "I don't think anything here will smell clean enough."

"I found some of your things in his workshop." He lifted her pack, as well as a small cloak. "I think this is Vivi's cloak. He must have stolen it from her."

"It's full of spell work," Melodie said, voice a little husky with sleep. "It glows."

"It does?" He jogged up the steps lightly and sat down shoulder to shoulder with her, handing her her things as he spread the cloak over them both.

"Hmm." She leaned her head against his shoulder. "It's the same glow that's on the shirt sleeves or collars of Kassia and Cervantes soldiers in the Illoa market square." She closed her eyes again.

"It's best you don't mention that to anyone else," he said, shifting to bring her closer against him.

"To protect the queen?" She nodded her head. "I know about keeping magical secrets."

"Maybe you and the queen can have a chat," Theo said.

"Mmm." She barely registered his words.

He tightened his hold and she thought he might have kissed the top of her head as she drifted off.

It wasn't a comfortable night, but she was warm under the cloak and with Theo's body heat, and when the sun rose, she refused to move, enjoying the warmth of the first rays of light on her outstretched legs.

"I don't want to go back in there." She stretched out the kinks, and then looked over at Theo.

"The sooner we get Marchant's things sorted, the sooner we can leave." Theo lifted her up with him as he stood, and she had to stamp her feet to ease the pins and needles.

She hated the thought of going back inside, but he was right. And if the people Marchant had taken through the years could be found, she had a duty to get that information.

They made tea in Marchant's kitchen and ate what they had left in their packs, then went back into the study to look it over more carefully in the light of day.

A tiny box on Marchant's desk suddenly gave a light ting of sound, and Melodie was about to pick it up to study it, when Theo made a sound of outrage.

"Here's a ledger." He held up a big, hardbound book which he'd opened to a neat row of names and numbers.

Melodie studied it. "First name, age, type of magic, amount, destination." She lifted her head. "He only gives the general area, not an exact address, or even who he sold the person to."

"Covering himself and them, no doubt. I can't think there would be a large number of people who had the funds or the inclination to enslave another, so he probably didn't need to detail their name and address. The general area told him exactly who he meant."

"There are over fifty names in this ledger." Melodie's hands shook as she set the book down. "Fifty people taken and sold."

Theo looked down and pointed to the first date. "It goes back more than thirty years."

Her father had tried to impress on her the horror of being forced to work for someone against her will, to keep her from exposing herself to danger, so she had imagined it many times. She didn't need to think about the terrible life every name on this list endured.

"I wish *I* could have killed him," she said.

"You helped," he said, brushing her cheek with his thumb.

She tilted her head back, about to say something rude, when the wooden floorboards began to vibrate beneath her boots.

She looked down. "What—?"

Theo lifted his head sharply, then set her away from him and ran out of the study.

Her gaze caught sight of the tiny box, and she suddenly understood.

Someone had triggered the web across the track.

Stupid. Stupid.

She raced after Theo, saw he'd gone straight out of the open front door, and leapt off the porch, heading straight for the forest.

"Stop!"

He turned, running backward as he faced her. "It has to be the Commander."

"The trap!"

Her words finally sunk in, and he stopped a few steps from the spell on the path that shone weakly in the morning light.

He look at the path, then turned back to her. Shook his head. "I forgot."

As he said it, a wall of riders emerged from the trees, and he spun to face them, hand out.

Gallain rode in the front line, as well as Jacinta, and Melodie saw a grim-faced man in his early forties in the center of the group.

They pulled up at the sight of Theo.

"There's a magical trap here. You need to go around." Theo pointed and the riders streamed forward, curving around the spot, and came to a stop in front of the house.

Melodie wondered who had tripped the web across the road. Gallain and the others knew about it. "If we hadn't already dealt with Marchant, he'd have been warned you were coming," she said.

Gallain shook his head. "One of the younger soldiers in the group apparently wasn't paying attention when that fact was relayed." He glanced back at someone, who squirmed in their saddle. "Why do you think we came in so fast? It was to give Marchant as little time as possible to react, if he was still around."

Theo jogged back, his whole demeanor relaxed as he called and joked with the mounted soldiers, until he reached the porch steps again.

"Commander." He put his fist over his heart as the grim-faced man slid from his horse.

Another, older soldier had dismounted as well, and he pulled Theo into a fierce hug. "Where's the bastard?" he asked.

"Dead." Theo pointed to the prison.

"And this is Melodie." The Commander was watching her, and he seemed less grim now. Perhaps because he knew Marchant was dead.

She gave a nervous nod.

"You gave yourself in exchange for my daughter," he said.

"For everyone," she corrected, and he gave a nod of acknowledgement.

As they spoke, most of the soldiers dismounted, and a slim woman moved to stand at the Commander's side.

It was a face she knew. A face she had never forgotten.

Melodie blinked. "Sue?"

"Avasu," the woman said. Then she climbed the steps and put her hands on Melodie's shoulders. "That's what my friends who are Venyatux call me."

"And other people?" Melodie asked.

"Other people call me Queen Ava of Kassia and Cervantes."

"I LOOKED FOR YOU AND YOUR FATHER FOR YEARS." AVA HAD HER arm through Melodie's and she tugged her a little way away from the buildings. "I offered your father a place to stay at my grand-mother's estate in Grimwalt, but he never came."

Melodie glanced behind her, grateful for a little time away from the curious stares and sidelong glances.

Ava would not countenance leaving Marchant's things to be stolen and used by those as bad as he was, and Melodie couldn't allow the soldiers to handle things she knew were dangerous, so she had personally sorted all the items into a useful pile and a dangerous pile.

In doing so, she had exposed her gift to all thirty of the Commander's unit, and she felt naked and vulnerable now.

Ava seemed to understand, and had suggested a walk while some of the men and women stacked the useful items onto Marchant's cart, to take back to Kassia and Cervantes, and others built a fire to burn the rest.

"My father sometimes wished he had taken you up on that offer, when times got hard for us." Melodie wondered what their lives would have been like if her father hadn't been so suspicious and stubborn.

Ava sighed. "I wish I had known you were living in Illoa."

"My father circled back there after years of wandering around Grimwalt, and when he died, I had no connections anywhere else."

"And you were too young to remember my full name." Ava shook her head, but Melodie laughed.

"Even if I had remembered it, I'd never have put it together with the queen of Kassia and Cervantes."

Ava made a face. "The thing that makes my blood run cold is that I should have realized that some people can see spell work. I knew you could. The fact that Marchant was wandering around looking at my shirts on soldiers makes me wonder who else knows."

"I think it was just him and me," Melodie said. "And he's dead." She touched Ava's arm. "And while our abilities were similar, I don't think they were the same."

"What do you mean?" Ava asked.

"I think he could see magic. I can see spell work. He could tell if someone had magical ability, and he could see the magic in a spell-worked item, but he couldn't discern the difference."

"So he saw Viviane's magic, but she tells me she was able to fool him into believing it was her cloak that he saw. And she wove a spell to hide her magic into her hair, and fooled him into thinking he was wrong about her magical ability." Ava spoke slowly.

"Yes. I can't see the magic inside someone. I can see the spell work woven into an item."

"But he didn't understand that." Ava glanced at her to confirm.

"He didn't. And I made sure he never did."

Ava stopped and turned to face her. "Can I persuade you to work in my court? Obviously there is an entire cohort that knows what you can do after this morning, but we can try to keep your ability as secret as possible."

Melodie glanced at her. "My father would strongly object."

Ava smiled. "I'm aware. I spoke to him about you on that journey." She lifted a hand to Melodie's shoulder. "How did he die?"

Melodie closed her eyes. "I saw a woman in the market square in Illoa, selling little wooden tokens. People were taking them, and then opening their purses and emptying everything in them into a hat she held out." She shook her head. "I tried to tell one of the men who'd just bought one that he was being cheated. I could see the spell work covering each token, but instead of confronting her, he turned and struck me. I fell to the ground and the woman started edging away. I watched her look very deliberately from me to him, and then she said: *Kill her*."

"And your father jumped between you?" Ava guessed.

Melodie nodded. "He had just come to look for me. He roared something and rushed forward just as the man pulled a knife from his boot and struck out at me."

"The crowd around us was suddenly galvanized and pulled him away, held him down. There were witnesses to the whole thing, but when the guards tried to find the woman, she was long gone. The man was sobbing when the guard took his token. He claimed he never meant to do anything to either me or my father." She sighed, shared a look with Ava. They both knew that he had been telling the truth.

"The woman sounds like someone I knew, back in the early days of the Rising Wave." Ava patted her hand in sympathy. "I know your father would be horrified, but you've always seemed to push against his strictures."

Melodie hesitated. "Theo says he'll help me help others. All those people my father wouldn't let me help, or who I wasn't able to warn. They weigh on me."

"We can work something out." Ava gave a slow nod. "We can call it fieldwork and palace duty."

Melodie liked the sound of that. "Did you see the ledger?" she asked. "Over fifty people like you and me, sold as slaves?"

"I saw." Ava's voice was quiet. "So fieldwork will definitely be part of it. You can move around Kassia and Cervantes, using that ledger, and find those people."

"What about in other countries? Marchant sold people all over the continent."

"I saw that." Ava's lips twisted. "We'll have to make a plan. Find people we trust to look into it."

Melodie searched her face, hoping she was being sincere.

"We won't leave them to rot," Ava promised her. They turned and headed back to the house. "I was like those people in the ledger at one time in my life. You would have become one, if Marchant got his way." She glanced over at Viviane, who along with Genevieve, Jon and Ricardo were helping to burn everything Melodie had judged dangerous in the fire that had been lit, throwing things into the flames with gusto. "As well as my daughter."

As they made their way across the lawn, Melodie saw Theo was standing with Ava's heart's choice, Luc Franck, near the porch, and both men turned and watched them approach.

They were both so clearly warriors, their faces so serious, their bodies so honed and dangerous, she suddenly felt flustered by the attention. Before she could help herself, she blurted out the first thing that came to mind. "Commander, did you know your sword is enspelled?"

There was a sudden silence all around her, and she glanced quickly to the side, and saw everyone in earshot had stopped what they were doing and were staring at her.

"Is it, now?" Luc Franck angled his sword away from him, looking down the length of the blade with interest.

She felt the heat rise in her cheeks. "Obviously, you already know that."

"Oh, no," Theo said, and there was a suspicious amusement in his voice. "He doesn't. What spell is it?"

She looked uncertainly between the two men, and then at Ava.

Ava gave her an encouraging smile.

"You must have noticed the blade is always sharp?" she said, tentatively.

"A blade that's always sharp," Luc Franck murmured. Then he looked up and smiled. Sent her a wink.

Ava gave a snort of amusement, and all around them, soldiers began to laugh.

Melodie turned in astonishment, trying to work out what was

going on, and Theo grabbed her up and swung her around, still chuckling.

"You have finally solved a very long-standing debate," he said, and kissed her on the lips before he set her down. He draped an arm over her shoulder and hugged her close. "I think you're truly one of us, now."

CHAPTER 37

MELODIE HAD NEVER BEEN to Ta-lin, that she remembered.

The center of Cervantes was small but charming, and a lot of it looked as if it had been built in the last fifteen years, since Kassia had fought the Rising Wave and lost.

"The old queen almost razed this place," Theo told her when she mentioned it. "So it's been rebuilt over time."

"Do you like it better than Fernwell?" she asked. She had always wanted to see the capital of Kassia, set in a glittering harbor, with a palace that people said shone in the morning light.

"I thought I would always prefer Ta-lin, but Fernwell is . . . vibrant. There's a lot happening there, whereas Ta-lin is sleepier. Slower-paced."

Melodie winced in her saddle and decided she wouldn't mind a slower pace for a bit.

They had barely rested since leaving Grimwalt, snatching a bit of sleep in tents. When they'd reached Illoa, Ava and Luc had spent an hour on the Grimwalt side, speaking to Grimwaldian officials, while everyone else had snatched a meal and a rest at the barracks on the other side of the river, and then they'd continued on, riding hard, stopping only to water the horses and eat.

"I only thought of it later, but while we were resting in Illoa, did you want to fetch your things from Vinest?" Theo asked.

She had thought about it, but she couldn't work out a way to do it that wouldn't have slowed the whole party down, and she had eventually decided there was nothing to go back for. "I can get new things," she said, and felt an easing of pressure at the words.

The past was behind her.

"Where do you stay when you're here?" she asked.

"At the official residence." He waved up ahead, and she saw a building rising up over the others in the wide street, nothing overtly ostentatious, but solid and gracefully proportioned.

She followed Theo through the arched entryway, where they were met by stable hands. Their group had broken up as soon as Talin had come into sight, some racing ahead, and it was controlled chaos in the big courtyard in front of the entrance.

She slid off her horse with relief, and held her bag awkwardly while Theo was pulled aside by someone who looked official.

He shook his head firmly at something that was said, and then turned to her, hand out. "Ava's given you one of the guest suites while they sort out a permanent arrangement for you. Roderick will show you the way, because apparently I have something I have to attend to."

The official-looking man's eyes widened at being designated as a guide, but he inclined his head cordially enough.

Theo took her hand, and as his warm fingers closed over hers, she regretted that they hadn't had a chance to speak much to each other over the last two days of wild riding, let alone anything else.

She missed the closeness. The connection she felt between them.

"I'll be up as soon as I can to see you."

She nodded, suddenly unable to speak, and then he walked away, swallowed by the chaos of horses and soldiers.

"This way." Roderick waved a hand toward the building, and she followed him up some stairs, along a passageway, and into what looked like a bedroom for visiting royalty.

"All right?" he asked.

She turned, taking it all in. "It seems like too much," she admitted.

"It's usually for heads of state, so enjoy." He grinned. "If the queen wants you here, she must like you. Can I get you anything else?"

She gave a nod. "I'd really like a bath."

He eyed her thoughtfully. "I'll arrange a bath and some food. Dinner is usually at seven, and it's very informal, but if that's all you have to wear, I'll find some clothes to send up to you, as well."

He left her with another incline of his head, and she sat at the window and looked out on the town, suddenly discombobulated at her new circumstances.

She had always looked at the Kassia and Cervantes soldiers and wished she had the same easy camaraderie and closeness they seemed to have with each other. Now she was in the bosom of the palace, in a room for visiting heads of state, and with a purpose that fulfilled what she'd wanted since she'd first seen the glow of spell work and understood what it was.

The food arrived first, and then the bath and clothing, and when she was fed, bathed and dressed, she realized she couldn't sit in the room any longer.

She ventured out and wandered the palace, learning the layout and enjoying its clean, simple lines.

She took a door outside and walked through a small garden and then out onto an older street that looked like it was an original part of the town. The little shops that lined it on either side were full of interesting wares, but she came to a stop in front of the goldsmith's.

She was studying the jewelry on display when she saw Theo walking toward her.

He stopped beside her, and unable to keep away, she sidled closer and slid her arm around his waist.

He went still for a beat, and then curved his arm along her shoulder.

"I couldn't find you," he said. His voice sounded a little frayed.

"I waited, but then I needed to move. I came onto this street by accident."

"Would you ever want to go back to this?" he asked, nodding toward the window.

"I enjoy it, so perhaps I can keep it as a hobby. Especially if I find items that can be used for protection." She had put her ring back on her finger, and she held it out.

"Dinner is usually in the hall," he said, tugging her back toward the palace. "But I organized a more private meal in your rooms for the two of us, if that suits you?"

"It does." She glanced up at him. Frowned. "Why do you seem nervous? Do you have bad news?" She remembered the hard shake of his head while he'd been talking to Roderick.

"That depends." He towed her through the arch into the garden, and down a path to a side entrance, and his grip on her hand tightened.

"Depends?" She stopped suddenly. "What's wrong?"

He made a noise, pulled her through the doorway, and lifted her against the wall under the stairs.

She looked down at him, shocked.

"Looks like you've evened up," he said. "Maybe even overtaken me."

Her eyes widened, and her cheeks burned as she realized what he was saying. Then she dipped her head and brushed her lips over his.

"I like it up here," she murmured, and kissed him again.

With a groan he let her slide down him to the ground, and pressed her back against the wall, hands braced on either side of her head. "The queen has made me head of your security."

She contemplated his words, then met his gaze. "That is something you want?"

"It is." He brushed a kiss to her throat. "I told you I would be the sword at your back, and now it's official."

"Official?" She worried her lower lip. Did that mean—?

"What is it?" He ran his thumb along her lip as if to soothe it.

"Can we still . . .?" She tried to think of the best way to say it.

"We haven't started yet." He grinned. "But yes."

"Well, that's all right then." She relaxed back against the wall. "How about we start now?"

NEW SERIES

Thank you for reading Truth's Blade. Subscribers to my new release notification list will be sent a copy of a bonus short story set just after Truth's Blade, of Theo and Melodie's first rescue mission. If you would like to receive the short story, please go to https://bookhip.com/WGSXPJR (a sign-up to the list will be required). I only send out newsletters when I have a new release or a giveaway, I will never share your information, and you can unsubscribe at any time.

Look out for the new Spell-worked Cage series, which is set in the same world as the Rising Wave. The first book will be out in 2025. Sign up to Michelle Diener's New Release Notification list by going to the link above, or to Michelle Diener's website (michellediener.com) to get reminders when there's a new release, bonus short stories and audiobooks, and more.

ALSO BY MICHELLE DIENER

FANTASY NOVELS BY MICHELLE DIENER

The Rising Wave series:

The Rising Wave (Prequel novella to THE TURNCOAT KING)

The Turncoat King

The Threadbare Queen

Fate's Arrow

Truth's Blade

Mistress of the Wind

The Dark Forest series:

The Golden Apple

The Silver Pear

SCIENCE FICTION NOVELS

Verdant String series:

Interference & Insurgency Box Set

Breakaway

Breakeven

Trailblazer

High Flyer

Wave Rider

Peace Maker

Enthraller

HISTORICAL FICTION NOVELS

A Dangerous Madness

Other historical novels:

Daughter of the Sky

SHORT PARANORMAL FICTION

Breaking Out: Part I (Short story)

Breaking Out: Part II (Novella)

To receive notification when a new book is released, and to receive
exclusive copies of numerous novellas and a free audio book, sign up at
michellediener.com.

ABOUT THE AUTHOR

Michelle Diener is an award winning author of historical fiction, science fiction and fantasy.

Michelle was born in London and currently lives in Australia with her husband and children.

You can contact Michelle through her website or sign up to receive notification when she has a new book out on her New Release Notification page.

Connect with Michelle
www.michellediener.com

ACKNOWLEDGMENTS

A huge thank you to as always to Claire and Jo, who help me make my stories the best they can be. Thank you to Jess, James, Tania, Nicole, Lynn, Barbara and Margaret in my Readers' Group for their feedback. Thank you also to Creative Paramita for the amazing cover.